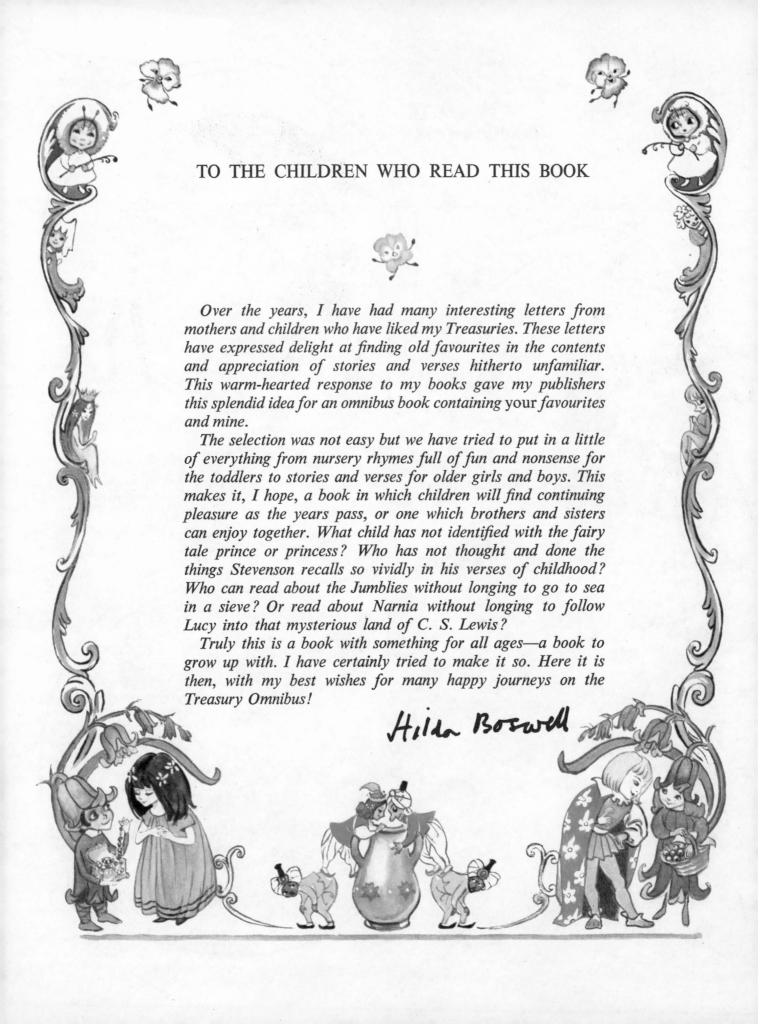

TO THE CHILDREN WHO READ THIS BOOK

Over the years, I have had many interesting letters from mothers and children who have liked my Treasuries. These letters have expressed delight at finding old favourites in the contents and appreciation of stories and verses hitherto unfamiliar. This warm-hearted response to my books gave my publishers this splendid idea for an omnibus book containing your favourites and mine.

The selection was not easy but we have tried to put in a little of everything from nursery rhymes full of fun and nonsense for the toddlers to stories and verses for older girls and boys. This makes it, I hope, a book in which children will find continuing pleasure as the years pass, or one which brothers and sisters can enjoy together. What child has not identified with the fairy tale prince or princess? Who has not thought and done the things Stevenson recalls so vividly in his verses of childhood? Who can read about the Jumblies without longing to go to sea in a sieve? Or read about Narnia without longing to follow Lucy into that mysterious land of C. S. Lewis?

Truly this is a book with something for all ages—a book to grow up with. I have certainly tried to make it so. Here it is then, with my best wishes for many happy journeys on the Treasury Omnibus!

Hilda Boswell

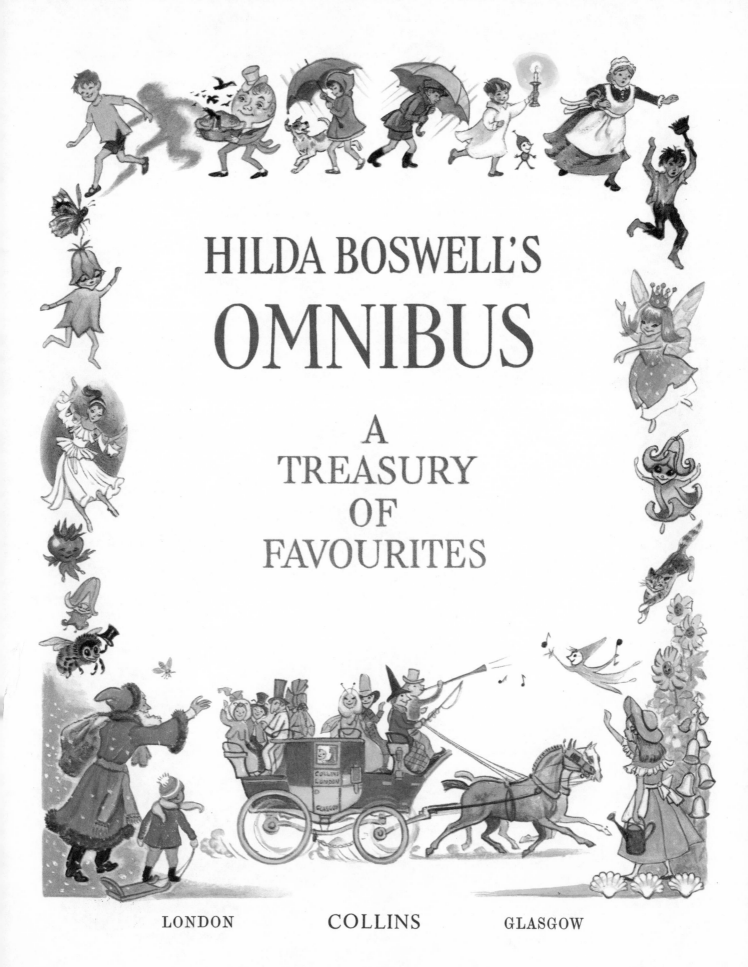

HILDA BOSWELL'S
OMNIBUS

A
TREASURY
OF
FAVOURITES

LONDON   COLLINS   GLASGOW

NURSERY RHYMES

FAIRY TALES

VERSES

STORIES

POEMS

First printed in this revised edition 1977
This impression 1978

ISBN 0 00 120308 8
Copyright © 1972 William Collins Sons and Co. Ltd.
Printed and made in Great Britain

FAVOURITE NURSERY RHYMES

Contents

	PAGE		PAGE
Ba-a, Ba-a, Black Sheep	12	Mary, Mary, Quite Contrary	20
Bobbie Shaftoe	49	Monday's Child	32
Come Let's to Bed	51	Old King Cole	22
Ding, Dong, Bell	38	Old Mother Hubbard	18
Fiddle-de-dee	50	One, Two, Buckle My Shoe	28
Goosey, Goosey, Gander	17	Oranges and Lemons	34
Handy-Pandy	42	Pat-a-Cake, Pat-a-Cake	26
Hark, Hark, the Dogs do Bark	8	Polly Put the Kettle on	10
Here We Go Round the Mulberry Bush	24	Pussy-Cat, Pussy-Cat	47
		Ride a Cock-Horse	21
Humpty Dumpty	13	Rub-a-Dub-Dub	16
I Had a Little Nut-Tree	30	Sing a Song of Sixpence	23
I Had a Little Pony	27	Simple Simon	37
I Saw a Ship a-Sailing	31	The North Wind Doth Blow	50
I Wish I Lived in a Caravan	29	The Old Person of Dover	54
Jack and Jill	14	The Owl and the Pussy-Cat	40
Jack Sprat	39	There Was an Old Man on the Border	52
Little Bo-Peep	44	There Was an Old Man with a Beard	53
Little Boy Blue	11	There Was an Old Woman	45
Little Jack Horner	48	There Was a Young Lady of Bute	55
Little Miss Muffet	15	Three Blind Mice	42
Little Polly Flinders	48	Tom, Tom, the Piper's Son	47
Mary Had a Little Lamb	43	Wee Willie Winkie	46

These rhymes and pictures first appeared in
Hilda Boswell's TREASURY OF NURSERY RHYMES

Hark, Hark, the Dogs do Bark

Hark, hark, the dogs do bark,
　　The beggars are coming to town;
Some in rags, some in jags,
　　And some in velvet gown.

YE WAY-FARERS REST

YE BOOK SHOP

Polly put the Kettle on

Polly, put the kettle on,
    Polly, put the kettle on,
Polly, put the kettle on,
       We'll all
          have
            tea.

Sukey, take it off again,
    Sukey, take it off again,
Sukey, take it off again,
       They've all
          gone
           away.

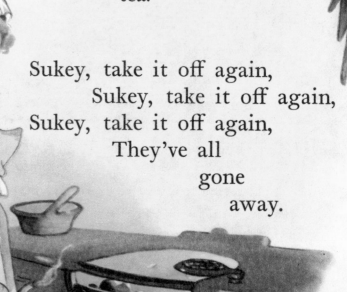

Little Boy Blue

Little Boy Blue, come blow your horn,
　The sheep's in the meadow,
The cow's in the corn.
　But where is the boy who looks after the sheep?
He's under the haystack, fast asleep.

Ba-a, Ba-a, black sheep

Baa, Baa, black sheep, have you any wool ?
Yes, sir, yes, sir, three bags full :
One for my master and one for my dame,
And one for the little boy
that lives
down
the
lane.

Humpty Dumpty

Humpty Dumpty sat on a wall,
Humpty Dumpty had a great fall;
All the King's horses and all the King's men
Couldn't put Humpty Dumpty
together again.

Jack and Jill

Jack and Jill went up the hill
　To fetch a pail of water;
Jack fell down and broke his crown,
　And Jill came tumbling after.

Up Jack got, and home did trot,
　As fast as he could caper;
He went to bed and plastered his head
　With vinegar and brown paper.

Little Miss Muffet

Little Miss Muffet
  Sat on a tuffet,
Eating her curds and whey;
  There came a great spider
  And sat down beside her,
  And frightened Miss Muffet away.

Rub-a-dub-dub

Rub-a-dub-dub,
　Three men in a tub,
And who do you think they be?

The butcher, the baker,
　The candlestick maker,
They all jumped out of a rotten potato,
　Turn 'em out, knaves all three!

Goosey, Goosey, Gander

Goosey, goosey, gander,
　Where shall I wander?
Upstairs, downstairs,
　In my lady's chamber.
There I met an old man
　Who wouldn't say his prayers,
I took him by his left leg,
　And threw him down the stairs.

Old Mother Hubbard

Old Mother Hubbard
Went to the cupboard,
    To get her poor Dog a bone;
But when she got there
    The cupboard was bare,
And so the poor Dog had none.

She went to the baker's
    To buy him some bread;
But when she came back
    The poor Dog was dead.

She went to the joiner's
    To buy him a coffin;
But when she came back,
    The poor Dog was laughing.

She took a clean dish
    To get him some tripe;
But when she came back,
    He was smoking a pipe.

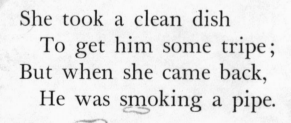

She went to the alehouse
  To get him some beer;
But when she came back,
  The Dog sat in a chair.

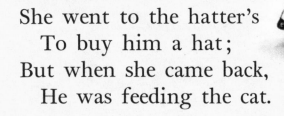

She went to the tavern
  For white wine and red;
But when she came back,
  The Dog stood on his head.

She went to the hatter's
  To buy him a hat;
But when she came back,
  He was feeding the cat.

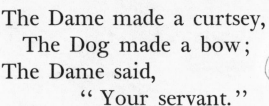

The Dame made a curtsey,
  The Dog made a bow;
The Dame said,
  " Your servant."
The Dog said,
  " Bow-wow!"

Mary, Mary, quite contrary

Mary, Mary, quite contrary,
How does your garden grow?
With silver bells and cockle shells,
And pretty maids all in a row.

Ride a Cock-Horse

Ride a cock-horse to Banbury Cross,
  To see a fine lady upon a white horse.
With rings on her fingers and bells on her toes,
  She shall have music wherever she goes.

Old King Cole

Old King Cole was a merry old soul,
  And a merry old soul was he.
He called for his pipe, and he called for his bowl,
  And he called for his fiddlers three.

Now every fiddler had a fine fiddle,
  And a very fine fiddle had he.
Tweedle, tweedle, tweedle-dee went the fiddlers,
  Tweedle, tweedle-dee.
Oh, there's none so fair, as can compare
  With King Cole and his fiddlers three.

Sing a Song of Sixpence

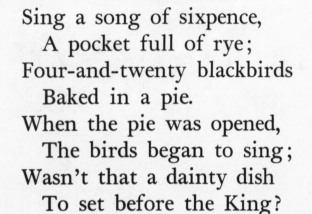

Sing a song of sixpence,
　A pocket full of rye;
Four-and-twenty blackbirds
　Baked in a pie.
When the pie was opened,
　The birds began to sing;
Wasn't that a dainty dish
　To set before the King?

The King was in the Counting-house,
　Counting out his money;
The Queen was in the parlour,
　Eating bread and honey.
The maid was in the garden,
　Hanging out the clothes;
When down came a blackbird,
　And pecked off her nose.

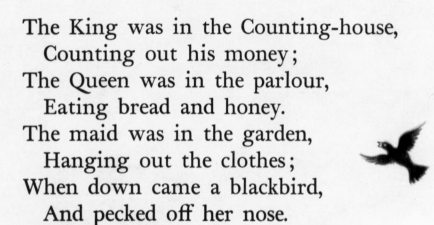

Here we go round the Mulberry Bush

Here we go round
   the mulberry bush,
The mulberry bush,
   the mulberry bush;
Here we go round
   the mulberry bush,
On a cold
   and frosty
     morning.

This is the way we wash our hands,
Wash our hands,
wash our hands;
This is the way we wash our hands,
On a cold
and frosty
morning.

This is the way we wash our clothes,
Wash our clothes,
wash our clothes;
This is the way we wash our clothes,
On a cold
and frosty
morning.

Pat-a-Cake, Pat-a-Cake

Pat-a-cake, pat-a-cake,
     baker's man!
So I will, master,
     as fast as I can;
Pat it and prick it
     and mark it
          with "T",
And put it in the oven
     for Tommy
          and
          me.

I had a Little Pony

I had a little pony,
     His name was Dapple-grey,
I lent him to a lady,
     To ride a mile away.

She whipped him, she lashed him,
     She rode him through the mire;
I would not lend
          my pony now,
          For all
               a lady's
               hire.

One, Two, buckle my shoe

One, Two, buckle my shoe,
   Three, Four, knock at the door,
Five, Six, pick up sticks,
   Seven, Eight, lay them straight,
Nine, Ten, the good fat hen.
   Eleven, Twelve, dig and delve,
Thirteen, Fourteen, maids a'courting,
   Fifteen, Sixteen, maids in the kitchen,
Seventeen, Eighteen, maids a'waiting,
   Nineteen, Twenty,
     my plate's
     empty.

I Wish I Lived in a Caravan

I wish I lived in a caravan,
   With a horse to drive, like a pedlar man!
Where he comes from nobody knows,
   Or where he goes to, but on he goes.
His caravan has windows too,
   And a chimney of tin that the smoke comes through;
He has a wife, with a baby brown,
   And they go riding from town to town.

I had a little nut-tree

I had a little nut-tree,
    nothing would it bear,
But a silver nutmeg and a golden pear;
The King of Spain's daughter
        came to visit me,
            And all was because
                of my little
                    nut-tree.

I saw a ship a-sailing

I saw a ship a-sailing,
        a-sailing on the sea;
And, oh! It was all laden
        with pretty things for thee!
There were comfits in the cabin
        and apples in the hold;
The sails were all of silk,
        and the masts were made of gold.
The four-and-twenty sailors
        that stood between the decks,
Were four-and-twenty white mice
        with chains about their necks.
The captain was a duck
        with a packet on his back;
And when the ship began to move,
        the captain said,
        " Quack! Quack!"

Monday's child
Is fair of face,

Tuesday's child
Is full of grace,

Wednesday's child
Is full of woe,

Thursday's child
Has far to go,

32

Friday's child
Is loving and giving,

Saturday's child works
Hard for his living,

And the child that is born on the Sabbath day,
Is bonny and blithe, and good and gay.

Oranges and Lemons

" Oranges and lemons,"
Say the bells of
St. Clement's.

" You owe me five farthings,"
Say the bells of St. Martin's.

" When will you pay me? "
Say the bells of Old Bailey.
" When I grow rich, "
Say the bells of Shoreditch.

"Pray, when will that be?"
Say the bells of Stepney.

"I do not know!"
Says the great bell of Bow.

Here comes a candle to light you to bed,
And here comes a chopper,
To chop off your
head.

Simple Simon

Simple Simon met a pie-man
  Going to the fair;
Said Simple Simon to the pie-man:
  " Let me taste your ware."
Said the pie-man to Simple Simon:
  " Show me first your penny."
Said Simple Simon to the pie-man:
  " Sir, I haven't any."

Ding, dong, bell

Ding, dong, bell, pussy's in the well.
  Who put her in? Little Johnny Green.
Who pulled her out? Little Tommy Stout.
  What a naughty boy was that,
To try to drown poor pussy cat,
  Who never did him any harm,
But killed the mice in his father's barn.

Jack Sprat

Jack Sprat could eat no fat,
His wife could eat no lean;
And so b'twixt them both you see,
They licked the platter clean.

The Owl and the Pussy-Cat

The owl and the pussy-cat went to sea
    In a beautiful pea-green boat.
They took some honey, and plenty of money
    Wrapped up in a five-pound note.
The owl looked up to the moon above,
    And sang to a small guitar,
" O lovely pussy! O pussy, my love !
What a lovely pussy you are, you are,
    What a lovely pussy you are ! "

Pussy said to the owl, "You elegant fowl!
    How wonderful sweet you sing!
O let us be married—too long we have tarried—
    But what shall we do for a ring?"
They sailed away for a year and a day
    To the land where the Bong-tree grows,
And there in a wood, a piggy-wig stood,
With a ring on the end of his nose, his nose,
    With a ring on the end of his nose.

"Dear pig, are you willing to sell for one shilling
    Your ring?" Said the piggy, "I will."
So they took it away, and were married next day
    By the turkey who lives on the hill.
They dined upon mince and slices of quince,
    Which they ate with a runcible spoon;
And hand in hand on the edge of the sand
They danced by the light of the moon, the moon,
    They danced by the light of the moon.

Three Blind Mice

Three blind mice, see how they run!
They all run after the farmer's wife,
Who cut off their tails
with the carving-knife.
Did ever you see

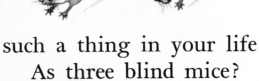

such a thing in your life
As three blind mice?

Handy-Pandy

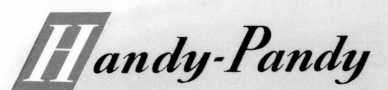

Handy-pandy, Jack-a-dandy,
Loved plum cake and sugar-candy;
He bought some at a grocer's shop,
And out he came,
      hop,
        hop,
          hop.

Mary had a little lamb

Mary had a little lamb,
  Its fleece was white as snow.
And everywhere that Mary went
  The lamb was sure to go.

It followed her to school one day,
  Which was against the rule;
It made the children laugh and play
  To see a lamb at school.

And so the teacher turned it out,
  But still it lingered near,
And waited patiently about
  Till Mary did appear.

  " What makes the lamb love Mary so? "
    The eager children cry.
  " Why, Mary loves the lamb, you know."
    And that's the reason why.

Little Bo-peep

Little Bo-peep has lost her sheep,
　And doesn't know where to find them,
Leave them alone, and they'll come home,
　Bringing their tails behind them.

　Little Bo-peep fell fast asleep,
　　And dreamt she heard them bleating;
　When she awoke, 'twas all a joke,
　　For they were still a-fleeting.

Then up she took her little crook,
　Determined for to find them;
She found them indeed,
　But it made her heart bleed,
For they'd left their tails behind them.

It happened one day,
　　　　as Bo-peep did stray
Into a meadow hard by,
Then she espied their tails,
　　　　　　side by side,
All hung on a tree to dry.

There was an old woman

There was an old woman,
Lived under a hill;
And if she's not gone,
She lives there still.

Baked apples she sold,
And cranberry pies,
And she's the old woman
Who never told lies.

Wee Willie Winkie

Wee Willie Winkie runs through the town,
  Upstairs and downstairs, in his nightgown;
Rapping at the window, crying through the lock,
  " Are the children in their beds?
    For now it's eight o'clock."

Pussy-cat, Pussy-cat

"Pussy-cat, pussy-cat,
　Where have you been?"
"I've been to London
　To visit the Queen."
"Pussy-cat, pussy-cat,
　What did you there?"
"I frightened a little mouse
　Under the chair."

Tom, Tom, the Piper's son

Tom, Tom, the Piper's son,
　Stole a pig, and away he run.
The pig was eat, and Tom was beat,
　And Tom went roaring down the street.

Little Jack Horner

Little Jack Horner sat in a corner,
   Eating his Christmas pie!
He put in his thumb,
   And pulled out a plum,
And said, " What a good boy am I ! "

Little Polly Flinders

Little Polly Flinders
   Sat among the cinders,
Warming her pretty little toes;
   Her mother came and caught her,
And whipped her little daughter,
   For spoiling her nice new clothes.

Bobbie Shaftoe

Bobbie Shaftoe's gone to sea,
Silver buckles at his knee;
When he comes back, he'll marry me,
Bonny Bobbie Shaftoe!

Bobbie Shaftoe's bright and fair,
Combing down his yellow hair,
He's my ain for evermair,
Bonny Bobbie Shaftoe.

The NORTH WIND DOTH BLOW

The north wind doth blow,
And we shall have snow,
And what will poor Robin do then, poor thing?
He'll sit in a barn,
And keep himself warm,
And hide his head under his wing,
                    poor thing.

FIDDLE-DE-DEE

Fiddle-de-dee, fiddle-de-dee,
The fly shall marry the humble-bee;
They went to church and married was she,
The fly has married the humble-bee.
Fiddle-de-dee, fiddle-de-dee!

Come let's to bed

"Come let's to bed," says Sleepy Head,
"Tarry awhile," says Slow.
"Put on the pan," says Greedy Nan,
"We'll sup before we go."

There was an old man on the Border

There was an old man on the Border,
Who lived in the utmost disorder;
He danced with the Cat, and made tea in his hat,
Which vexed all the folks on the Border.

THERE WAS AN OLD MAN WITH A BEARD

There was an old man with a beard,
Who said, " It is just as I feared!—
Two Owls and a Hen, four Larks and a Wren,
Have all built their nests in my beard! "

The Old Person of Dover

There was an old person of Dover,
Who rushed through a field of blue clover;
But some very large bees stung his nose and his knees,
So he very soon went back to Dover.

There was a Young Lady of Bute

There was a young lady of Bute,
Who played on a silver-gilt flute;
  She played several jigs
    to her Uncle's white pigs,
      That amusing
        young lady
          of Bute.

FAVOURITE FAIRY TALES

*Some of the best-known and best-loved fairy tales
simply retold for the youngest children*

Contents

		PAGE
Hansel and Gretel	THE BROTHERS GRIMM	57
The Wild Swans	HANS ANDERSEN	66
Tom Thumb	TRADITIONAL	72
Rapunzel	THE BROTHERS GRIMM	82
Goldilocks and the Three Bears	TRADITIONAL	90
Snow White and the Seven Dwarfs	THE BROTHERS GRIMM	97

These illustrated fairy tales first appeared in
Hilda Boswell's TREASURY OF FAIRY TALES

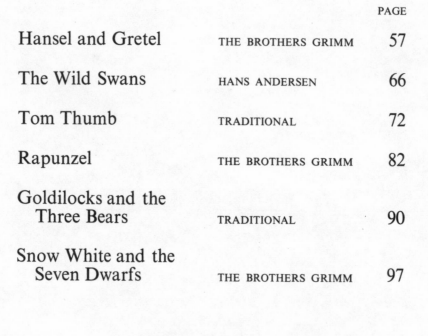

HANSEL AND GRETEL

HANSEL and Gretel lived with their father, who was a woodcutter, in a little hut at the edge of a forest. For a long time they were very happy. They would go off with their father in the early morning and stay near him while he worked. The two children collected berries and nuts and mushrooms, or picked bunches of wild flowers. Gretel was clever at weaving and she made little baskets from dried grasses.

But all this was changed when their father married again, for their stepmother was cruel, and thought nothing the children did was right. She was a greedy woman, too, and began to complain and to say that there was not enough food, and that the children must go. One night, as he lay awake in his little bed, Hansel heard his father sadly agree to take the children into the forest and lose them. Hansel waited until the very early

morning, and then, before the others were awake, he crept out of the little hut and filled his pockets with small white pebbles.

That day, when they were deep in the forest, the father said, " You must wait here until I come back."

The children waited until it grew dark and cold, and at last Gretel said, " He must have forgotten all about us."

Then Hansel told her of all that his stepmother had said.

" But never mind! " said Hansel. " I have left a trail of little white pebbles along the way we came, and as soon as the moon is up, we shall be able to find our way home."

When the horrid stepmother opened the door of the hut, there were the two children, waiting to come in. She smiled and pretended to be pleased to see them, and

only scolded them for straying away from their father.

The next night Hansel again heard his father agree to take the children with him, and to lose them.

"Take them deeper into the wood this time," scolded the woman. "We cannot go on feeding them for ever. They must find their own way in the world."

Sadly the father did as he had promised, and they walked until the two children were weary and could go no farther. Then the father made a splendid bonfire, and the children lay down under a tree and were soon fast asleep. When they awoke the fire was out and the man was already miles away.

"Never mind!" said Hansel. "We shall be able to find our way, for although the door was locked and I could not go out to collect pebbles, I had some crusts in my pocket, and I have made a trail with them."

It was already early morning, and the two children

set off, hand in hand; but there were no crumbs left, for the birds had flown down and eaten them.

Gretel began to cry, but Hansel said, "Look, Gretel! Do you see the smoke rising above those trees? There must be a woodman's hut there. We will go and ask for food."

The children followed the direction of the smoke and presently found themselves in a little clearing, and there stood a dear little house!

Hansel and Gretel ran up to it, and were just going to knock when they saw that the door was made of chocolate.

"We need not be hungry any more," said Gretel.

"Look!" said Hansel. "The walls of the house are made of gingerbread, and the window-frames are barley sugar!" And both the children burst out laughing.

Out popped a little old woman from the door.

" What jolly children! " she said. " Come in, my dears, there are more good things inside."

Happily Hansel and Gretel followed her into the little house. The old woman set the table and gave them a good meal. She seemed to have a store of everything children like, in her cupboards, and after they had eaten the old woman led them upstairs into a pretty bedroom and said: " You shall rest here, my dears, and when you are ready we will have another meal."

After a few days of such kindness, and such good food, Hansel and Gretel began to grow quite plump.

One morning, Gretel woke to find that Hansel's bed was empty.

" Where is my brother? " she asked the old woman.

" Get on with your work! I shall want a great heap of firewood, for I must make the oven nice and hot," said the old woman.

When Gretel was outside the cottage she heard Hansel crying, and looking around, she found him tied up in the hen-house. She told Hansel that the old woman had given orders for the oven to be made ready.

Hansel said to his sister: "You must help the old woman. Do not say that you have found me, but do as she asks."

Then Gretel bent down, in case the old woman was somewhere nearby, and Hansel told her what to do.

Gretel ran off, and all day long she collected wood!

Every now and then she would say to the old woman: "I do wonder where Hansel can have got to?" and the old woman would chuckle as if she had a splendid secret, but she did not reply.

Towards evening, when Gretel was almost too tired to work any longer, and the fire was so strong and bright that the heat in the little kitchen was unbearable, the old woman said: "Good! It is hot enough now. The oven is ready."

"Are you going to roast a goose?" asked Gretel.

"Yes, my dear, a nice, plump, little goose," laughed the old woman.

"But surely," said Gretel, "you never mean to put a goose in the oven without finding out first whether the heat is too little or too much? You might scorch it and then your supper would be spoilt."

"H'm!" said the old woman. "It is quite a clever child! I should never have thought of that!" and she opened the oven door and popped her head inside, just to see whether or not it was the right heat.

Quick as lightning, Gretel seized the old woman, and with one tremendous heave she thrust her inside the oven and slammed the door. Then she ran out to Hansel and set him free.

" Let us run into the wood and hide! " said Hansel.

" But we cannot leave the old woman in the oven! "
said Gretel.

" She is cruel, like a bad witch," said Hansel; but
Gretel led him back to the kitchen, where the old woman
was crying and begging to be let out.

" Will you be good, for always and always? " asked
Gretel.

" I *will* be good for always and always! " said the
old woman.

" Will you never be unkind to any child who may
knock on the door? " asked Hansel.

" Never—never—never! " sobbed the old woman.

" Then if I may have your magic stick you shall come
out," asked Hansel.

" Take it! " said the old woman. " It is behind the

door. The stick will obey you always, and it will turn all that it touches into nice things to eat; toffee or sponge-cake, gingerbread or chocolate, just as you wish.''

So Gretel unlatched the oven door, and Hansel helped the old woman out, and after that she was no trouble.

Sometimes Hansel would say to the stick: '' Fetch my father here! '' and the stick would run out, and almost at once the woodcutter would knock on the door, and say: '' Do Hansel and Gretel live in this little house? ''

Then they would have a lovely day together; but, of course, neither Hansel nor Gretel ever invited the step-mother!

The WILD SWANS

IN a far-off country dwelt a King who had eleven sons and one daughter, a beautiful child called Elise. The children loved each other and were very happy until the day came when their father, the King, married a very wicked Queen. She sent Elise off into the country to be brought up by peasants, and told the King so many falsehoods about the poor Princes that he took no more interest in them and allowed her to drive them from the palace.

" Go out into the world! " she cried after them. " Go in the form of great speechless birds! "

Immediately the brothers changed into eleven beautiful white swans which flew off above the tree-tops.

Time passed, and when Elise was fifteen years old the King asked for her to return home. When the Queen saw how beautiful she was, she was filled with hatred, and before presenting her to the King, she smeared the maiden's face with walnut juice until it looked quite swarthy, and so entangled her hair that the King was shocked to see such an ugly creature and swore it could not be his daughter.

Poor Elise crept away into the forest and wept; and thought of her eleven brothers. Then she bathed in a nearby stream so that she regained her former beauty.

In the forest she met an old woman. Elise asked her if she had seen eleven princes ride through the wood. "No," replied the old woman, "but I saw eleven swans with gold crowns on their heads." And she took Elise to the place where she had seen the strange birds. Elise thanked the old woman and settled down to wait. Then, just as the sun was sinking, the eleven swans appeared, flying one behind the other. They came to rest beside Elise and flapped their long white wings. As the sun sank behind the trees the swans disappeared and in their place stood the eleven brothers.

"When the sun is above the horizon," explained the eldest brother, "we are swans; but as soon as it sets we regain our human form." The princes now lived in a far-off land, and they began to make plans to

take their sister back with them.

In the morning, when they were once again transformed into birds, the eleven brothers placed Elise on a mat which they had woven during the night from willow bark, and taking the four corners in their beaks, they flew away with her across the sea.

At last they reached the kingdom where the brothers lived, and they took her to a cave where she might sleep comfortably after her long journey. As she slept she had a strange dream. She dreamt that a fairy came and told her how she might free her brothers from the wicked spell.

" But," said the fairy, " you must have courage and patience. Do you see those stinging nettles which grow outside this cave? You must pluck and weave them into eleven shirts for your brothers. This will free them from the spell, but there is one condition—while you are engaged on this work no word must pass your lips."

When Elise awoke in the morning she at once set to work to gather the stinging nettles, although they blistered her hands painfully. Then she trampled on the nettles with her naked feet and spun the green yarn. All day and all night she worked, for she could not rest until she had freed her brothers. The following day, when three shirts had been completed, Elise heard the sound of a hunting horn in the forest. The sound came nearer, and presently the King of that country, with his hunters, stood at the entrance to the cave. The King was so

struck by Elise's beauty that he wanted to make her his Queen. In spite of her tears and dumb protests (for, of course, she did not dare utter a word), she was carried off to the palace and dressed in the most beautiful and costly clothes. Now she looked more lovely than a vision and the King loved her even more tenderly than before.

Elise was grief-stricken for the fate of her brothers until one day she discovered in a cellar of the palace the three shirts which she had made and the bundle of green nettle yarn. One of the King's men had carried them from the cave. Every night after that she stole down to the cellar when the palace was asleep and worked all through the small hours on the remaining eight shirts.

One night, when she had finished the seventh shirt, the Archbishop saw her leave the cellar. Quietly he waited until she had returned to her own room and then he crept into the cellar and saw the shirts and the heap of nettle yarn. He went straight to the King and told him everything he had seen, whispering that the Queen must indeed be a witch and should be burnt at the stake.

The King wept bitterly, but since Elise did not utter a word in her own defence, he was powerless to save her. The guard took her away and locked her in the very cellar where the shirts and the nettles were, to await the day of execution. Elise wept for joy to find herself there and set feverishly to work upon the remaining four shirts. For two nights and a day she worked without ceasing, and just as she was finishing the last shirt the guard came to summon her. Grasping the eleven shirts, she was bundled into a cart and carried out through the palace gates. Just then eleven white swans appeared in the sky, and as they approached Elise recognised her brothers. They alighted on the cart beside her and quickly she threw the eleven shirts over them. Immediately they were changed into eleven handsome princes.

" Now I can speak! " cried Elise. " I am innocent."

" Yes, she is innocent! " said her eldest brother, and told the whole story.

The King cried for joy and took the fair Elise in his arms, happy to have his Queen back once more; and Elise was happy too, for now she had not only a very kind and handsome husband whom she loved, but she also had her eleven dear brothers restored to her.

Tom Thumb

AN old man and his wife sat by the open window
of their cottage one summer's evening.

"It is getting too dark to see," said the old
man. "Time to go to bed."

"I have just finished. What do you think of this?"
said his wife, and she held up a baby's bonnet, beautifully
worked with fine, small stitches.

"It is well done," said the old man; "but you know
it would give me real pleasure if it could have been for
our own child."

The old woman sighed, for she had always wanted
children of her very own. Instead she spent her time in
sewing pretty things for every new baby who came to
the village.

"Yes," she said now, "I should have been happy, too,

if we had even only one child; even if it should be as small as my thumb."

Outside the window they heard a peal of silvery laughter.

"That wasn't a bird," said the old man. "Come to bed, wife!" So they closed the window and went upstairs.

The fairy, for it was a fairy who had heard them talking, flew back to fairyland and told the Queen about the little old woman who would welcome a baby no bigger than her thumb.

"If she is a good woman she shall have her child," said the Queen, and waved her magic wand.

The next morning, when the old woman woke, there beside her lay the most perfect little boy she had ever seen. He had bright, brown eyes and a mop of curly

hair, and he lay there chuckling and laughing, as merry as could be . . . and he was exactly the size of the old woman's thumb! She was overjoyed, and now busied herself in making the tiniest and finest baby clothes anyone had ever seen. The baby was so small that she made him a cradle from a pea-pod, and lined it each day with fresh flower petals.

They were poor old people, but she had saved for years the small scraps left over from the sewing she had done for others, and now all these were put to good use, and Tom Thumb, for that was his name, was finely dressed. The old woman even used rose petals to line his cloth bonnets, and plaited fine grasses to make shoes for his small feet.

Everyone came from miles around to see this little boy, who never grew any bigger. He could sing and talk, though his voice was no louder than that of a mouse, and he was full of fun, but the school-mistress found she could not have him in school, for when he was there the children never did any lessons! Tom Thumb would sit in a little box on the teacher's desk, and whenever her back was turned, he would balance on the ink-well or slide down the ruler and make the children laugh!

He kept the old man and woman very busy, for he was always up to tricks, and he was so tiny that he could hide in all sorts of small corners. They often lost sight of him for hours at a time. Sometimes he was allowed to go farther from home in the old man's pocket, and then his mother would dress Tom Thumb in a scarlet coat and cap, so that he could be more easily seen, if he strayed.

One day the old man went fishing, and Tom Thumb begged to go too.

"Very well," said his mother; "but be a good boy and stay close to your father, or a big fish will swallow you up."

"Even a little fish could swallow Tom Thumb," laughed the old man, as they set off. He was so busy with his work, and so un- used to having Tom Thumb with him by the river- side, that the old man soon forgot all about him, and it was not until it was time to return home that he dis- covered there was no sign any- where of little Tom Thumb.

He called and called, and he searched until it was almost too dark to see his way home, but he could find no trace of him—not even his scarlet cap.

Sadly he returned to the old woman, who had a fine supper waiting, and was ready to scold him for keeping the little boy out so late, but when she saw that he came alone she burst into tears.

" I expect the fairies took him. He must have been a gift from the fairies in the first place, and I suppose they have taken him back," said the old man.

" No! No! " cried the old woman. " You forgot him. I know you did. And poor Tom Thumb has fallen into the river and been swallowed by a fish."

The old woman was right, for Tom had gone off to explore the river's bank, and, slipping in the mud, had fallen in, and almost at once had been swallowed by an

enormous fish. It was very dark and warm inside, but Tom was not uncomfortable and he soon fell asleep.

Now this fish was so *enormous* that the man who caught it said to himself: " A splendid fish indeed! Good enough for the King! And as he was passing that way, he called in at the Palace and gave it to the Royal cook.

Tom Thumb did not wake up until the fish, coated with shrimp sauce and trimmed with lemon and parsley, was set before the King on a silver dish, and then, as the fish was cut open, he sat up, feeling very hot and stuffy, and red in the face, and waved his cap.

" Hey, there! What are you doing, waking me up like that? " shouted Tom, and the King and Queen and all the Lords and Ladies burst out laughing at the sight of the comical little fellow. The King set him on the rim of his wine-glass, and fed him dainty morsels on the end of a pin, and let him dance about the table, and swing from the flowers. Tom, who was never shy, had a splendid time, and was quite content to stay in the Palace as long as people were kind to him.

The King had a special little chair made for him, from solid silver, with tiny red velvet cushions, and Tom sat in this chair, close to the King's plate, at every meal. He had a little house of his own, like a doll's house, only much finer, in the Palace grounds, and the furniture in it was copied from the Queen's own designs. Tom wore clothes of satin and velvet and even carried a tiny golden sword—not that it was sharp enough to cut anything— for the King was afraid Tom might hurt himself. For a time Tom was very happy, but he soon found that the King treated him as a toy; like a little clown who could be wound up, to hop and skip and dance, and to make people laugh.

It was very tiring trying to keep the King and Queen amused. Tom did not like it when the ladies of the Court picked him up and petted him as though he were some sort of small, tame animal; they even knelt down on the grass before the windows of his little house

and peeped in at him; and once when he had drawn the curtains, the Queen was very angry. So poor Tom began to wish he could be back in the cottage with his own mother and father.

He grew pale and thin, and did not laugh or sing or dance any more, and he tried hard to think of some way in which he could get back home again.

One day the King said to the Queen: "I am tired of the little fellow. He has grown very dull. What shall we do with him?"

The Queen thought for a long while, and then she said:

" I think the best thing would be to give him to some kind country folk to care for. We could pay them well, of course."

" Good! " said the King. " Then we could have him at the Palace on special occasions; that would be far more amusing than seeing him every day."

Tom began to cheer up when he heard this, and he jumped out of the Queen's wardrobe, where he had been hiding, and danced all about the room.

" Oh, so you have heard, have you? " laughed the King. " Very well, little fellow, you shall have one wish before you leave the Palace."

The Queen sighed, thinking that Tom, who was by this time very spoilt, would be sure to choose something like a dozen servants, or a bag of diamonds. She was so surprised and pleased when Tom said:

" I should like to go home."

The King was pleased, too, and he had all Tom's things carefully packed and went himself to the cottage of the old man and his wife, who were so very happy to see Tom again that they gladly forgave him for staying away so long. They agreed to take Tom to the Palace twice a year on the King's and the Queen's birthdays, and to take great care of him for the rest of his life.

The old man and woman were never tired of hearing of Tom's adventures, and each time he returned he had fresh things to tell them, so they were never dull, and they all lived happily together in the little cottage.

RAPUNZEL

THERE was once, long ago, a beautiful girl called Rapunzel who had long golden hair which she wore in a long plait. When Rapunzel was a baby a wicked witch had stolen her from her mother and father and had shut her up in a tower which stood in a wood. It had neither staircase nor doors, but only a little window high up in the wall.

When the witch wanted

to enter the tower, she stood at the foot of it and shouted:

"Rapunzel, Rapunzel,
let down your hair."

Then Rapunzel would let down her long golden plait and the witch would climb up by it and go in through the window.

Rapunzel was very lonely all day in the tower and often she would sing a plaintive song to pass away the time. One day a Prince rode by the tower and heard her sweet song. Immediately he fell in love with her beautiful voice and made up his mind that some day he would marry the lady who could sing like that. But although he longed to meet her, he could see no way of getting into the tower.

"There's no door and no staircase," he thought to himself sadly, and he rode away through the forest again.

But the voice of Rapunzel haunted the

Prince and every day he rode back to the tower to hear it.
One day while he was hiding behind some trees, he saw
the witch approach. He saw her come to the foot of the
tower and heard her cry:

"Rapunzel, Rapunzel,
  let down your hair."

Then he watched in amazement as Rapunzel lowered her
hair from the window and the witch climbed up.

Next day he rode to the tower, as it began to grow
dark, and called softly:

"Rapunzel, Rapunzel,
  let down your hair."

Down came Rapunzel's golden plait and the King's son climbed up by it.

At first Rapunzel was frightened, but the Prince talked to her so kindly that she soon lost her fear. He told her that he had fallen in love with her and wanted to marry her.

" But how can I get down from this tower? " asked poor Rapunzel.

" Next time I come I will bring a rope, " said the Prince. " Do not despair. I will help you down and my horse can carry both of us away to my palace where the witch will never find us. "

Now Rapunzel's song was happy as she waited and watched for her Prince to come back. But alas, the wicked witch had seen the Prince leave the tower and guessed that

he was planning to take Rapunzel away.

She flew into a furious rage and when she got into the tower she cut off Rapunzel's beautiful hair with an enormous pair of scissors.

"You will never see your fine Prince again!" she shouted at the poor girl.

Then she sent Rapunzel away into the dark forest and she herself hid in the tower until the Prince returned.

When she heard him call:

"Rapunzel, Rapunzel, let down your hair,"

she threw down one end of the long plait while she held the other tightly.

The Prince climbed up the rope, but instead of seeing the beautiful Rapunzel waiting for him at the top, he saw the face of the ugly old witch.

"Ah," she cried mockingly, "you have come to fetch Rapunzel, but you will never see her again."

The Prince was beside himself with grief and in his despair he sprang out of the window. At the foot of the tower was a thorny bush and as the Prince landed on it the thorns hurt his eyes and he became blind.

But he couldn't believe that his lovely Rapunzel was dead and, although he could not see, he set out to search for her. Day

after day he rode in the forest, asking people if they had seen a beautiful fair lady. But no one had.

Then one day as he sat resting in the shade of a large tree, he heard a voice singing. The Prince raised his head, then got up, turning from one side to another to find out from which direction the sound was coming.

For the song was none other than the same sad song

that he had heard Rapunzel sing in the tower. And he knew, without a doubt, that the singer could only be his own dear Rapunzel.

He began to call her name: "Rapunzel! Rapunzel!"

Rapunzel had been living in the forest in great poverty but she thought constantly of her handsome Prince and wondered what had become of him. When she heard his voice calling her name she ran towards the sound and soon saw her Prince whom she had despaired of ever seeing again.

She ran to him and threw her arms around his neck. When she discovered that he was blind, she wept and two of her tears fell on his eyes.

Immediately his eyes became better and he could see again.

Then the Prince took Rapunzel away from the forest, riding his great, white, galloping horse. They rode away to the Prince's own kingdom where they were received with joy, and they lived long and happily together.

GOLDILOCKS and the THREE BEARS

THERE was once a little girl called Goldilocks who lived in a house near a wood with her mother and father. She was called Goldilocks because she had the most beautiful long hair which fell to her waist in soft curls. She had big blue eyes, a turned-up nose and rosy-red lips.

One warm summer's day Goldilocks went into the woods to gather some flowers. Her mother and father had often warned her not to stray too far from home in case she got lost, and usually Goldilocks stayed near her own garden. But this day she was feeling adventurous and a little bit naughty, so she decided to explore the woods. She wandered among the trees for a while and, just when she was beginning to realise that she was lost, she came upon a pretty cottage standing in a clearing.

" What a dear little house! " said Goldilocks. " I have never seen it before. I wonder who lives there? "

She was a very curious little girl so she went up to the house and knocked at the door. No one came. She opened the door and went in. In the first room she came to she saw three bowls of porridge set on the table. There was a great big bowl, a medium-sized bowl and a tiny little bowl. The porridge smelled so good that it made Goldilocks feel quite hungry. She tried the porridge in the great big bowl but it was too hot. She tried the porridge in the medium-sized bowl but it was too cold. Then she tried the porridge in the tiny little bowl and it was just right, so she ate it all up.

When she had finished she noticed that in front of the fire stood three chairs, a large chair, a medium-sized chair and a tiny little chair.

Goldilocks sat in the large one but it was too hard. She tried the middle one but it was too soft. But the little

chair was just right so Goldilocks sat down in it until—*bang*—the bottom of the chair fell out and she landed on the floor.

"I wonder what is upstairs," thought Goldilocks as she picked herself off the floor. "I'll go up and see."

In the bedroom upstairs were three beds—an enormous bed, a medium-sized bed and a tiny little bed. The biggest bed was too hard and the middle bed was too soft, but the tiny little bed was just right.

Goldilocks felt very sleepy and she lay down on it. It was so comfortable that soon she fell fast asleep.

By-and-by the owners of the cottage came home. They were three bears—a Daddy Bear, a Mummy Bear and a Baby Bear. They had been shopping at a nearby village and now they were feeling very tired and hungry. They were looking forward to eating their porridge and to having a nice long rest. But as soon as they came in, they noticed that things weren't exactly as they had left them and that someone had been in their house.

In the biggest bowl of porridge there was a spoon, and the medium-sized bowl had finger-marks all over it.

" Who's been eating *my* porridge? " growled Daddy Bear.

" Who's been eating *my* porridge? " cried Mummy Bear.

" And who's been eating *my* porridge? " squeaked Baby Bear, " and has eaten it all up! "

Then the Bear family noticed something wrong with

their fireside chairs. The biggest chair was out of position and a cushion from the medium-sized chair lay on the floor.

"Who's been sitting in *my* chair?" growled Daddy Bear.

"Who's been sitting in *my* chair?" cried Mummy Bear.

"And who's been sitting on *my* chair?" squeaked Baby Bear. "They've broken it to pieces!"

Then the bears decided to go upstairs to look around because they thought that thieves had been in their house. They went into the bedroom and right away they noticed that the biggest bed was all rumpled, and the sheets and blankets on the

medium-sized bed were very untidy. They *were* annoyed.

"Who's been lying on *my* bed?" growled Daddy Bear.

"Who's been lying on *my* bed?" cried Mummy Bear.

"And who's been lying on *my* bed?" squeaked Baby Bear. "And look—she's still there! It's a little girl!"

At the sound of their voices Goldilocks woke up with a start. What a fright she had to see the three bears looking down on her!

But they were kind bears although they looked so fierce and when Goldilocks said she was sorry to have gone into their house, they forgave her. They said she could come back and see them often and Goldilocks was very pleased.

Then Daddy Bear took Goldilocks home, while Mummy Bear and Baby Bear stood at the cottage door waving good-bye to her.

SNOW WHITE and the SEVEN DWARFS

ONCE upon a time in a far-away land there lived a pretty little princess called Snow White. She had a skin as white as snow, hair as black as ebony and lips as red as cherries.

Her mother the Queen had died when she was quite young and some time afterwards her father the King married another wife and brought her to the palace. The new Queen was very beautiful but she was so proud and haughty that she could not bear anyone to be prettier than herself. She owned a wonderful, magic mirror, and when she stepped before it and said:

> " Oh, mirror, mirror, on the wall,
> Who is the fairest of us all? "

it replied:

> " Thou art the fairest, lady Queen."

But little Snow White was growing prettier and prettier

as each day passed, and one day when the Queen spoke to her mirror it made a different answer:

"O Queen, thy loveliness is rare,
But Snow White seems to all more fair."

The Queen immediately flew into a furious rage and

resolved in her heart that Snow White must die. So she called one of her huntsmen and ordered him to take the little princess into the huge forest which surrounded the palace, and leave her there to die. The huntsman was a kindly man and was most unwilling to do this cruel deed, but he was too afraid of the Queen to disobey her commands.

He took Snow White into the forest, but instead of

leaving her in the heart of the dense woods, he took her to a part which was not so thickly wooded and left her there.

Poor little Snow White was very frightened alone in the woods. Darkness was falling and although she was not in the thickest part of the wood, she was still lost, lonely and afraid. She started to run blindly between the tall trees and just when she felt that she couldn't go on any farther, she came upon a clearing where there stood a little cottage.

Snow White tapped timidly on the cottage door to ask

for shelter for the night, but no one came. She knocked again a bit louder but still there was no reply. Eventually she pushed the door cautiously and found that it was not locked. Inside, the cottage was small but very clean and tidy. There was a table neatly set with seven little plates, seven little knives and seven little forks. Beside the fire were seven little chairs and on the other side by the wall were seven little beds.

Snow White was hungry so she ate some bread from each of the little plates, and then she felt so sleepy that she lay down on one of the little beds. Immediately she fell fast asleep, and didn't even wake when the owners of the cottage came home.

They were seven little dwarfs who dug for ore all day in the mountains. Every night they came home to their cottage in the wood, tired and hungry, looking forward to a meal and a long sleep.

They were angry when they discovered that someone had come into their cottage while they were out, and even angrier to find that some bread had been eaten from each of their plates. But when they came upon Snow White sleeping peacefully in one of their beds they could not be angry any longer for they had never seen such a beautiful girl in all their lives before. They shook her gently to awaken her, and when she told them about how the wicked Queen had tried to kill her, they felt very sorry and said she might stay with them for as long as she wanted.

" You can wash our clothes, and cook our food and clean our cottage," they told her, " but you must remember that while we are away in the mountains all day, you must not let *anyone* in the cottage. For if your wicked

stepmother finds out that you still live, she may try to harm you again.''

Snow White loved keeping house for the seven dwarfs and for a long time she lived happily with them, always remembering never to let anyone come into the cottage. But one day she was feeling rather bored and when an old woman came to the door selling apples, she forgot the dwarfs' warning, and asked her to come in. ''For what harm can an old woman do to me?'' thought Snow White.

But Snow White did not know that the old woman was none other than her wicked stepmother in disguise. The Queen had discovered from the magic mirror that Snow White was not dead but was living with the dwarfs in the forest. Immediately she had started to make plans, wondering how she could get rid of her stepdaughter. At last she had had an idea. She would poison an apple, disguise herself as an old woman and take the apple to Snow White. She chose a lovely shining, rosy-red apple which she knew the Princess would be unable to resist, and set off for the cottage in the forest.

Snow White accepted the apple with delight, and it looked so fresh and rosy that she took a great bite from it. Immediately she fell down, as though she were dead, and the wicked Queen went away, laughing gleefully because her plans had gone so well.

When the dwarfs came home at the

end of the day, they were heartbroken to see Snow White lying so still and so white on the floor.

"We cannot bury her in the cold ground," said one.

"Oh, no!" the rest of them chorused.

"Let us make a glass case," said another. "We shall place her in it and everyone who passes may see the beautiful princess."

The dwarfs all agreed to do this and set about building a beautiful glass case. This done, they laid Snow White in it very tenderly, and carried it to the top of a high hill.

Some time after, a Prince was riding by and when he saw Snow White he immediately fell deeply in love with her. He begged the dwarfs to let him take her back to his Palace with him, and when they realised how much he loved their dear Snow White, they agreed.

They helped the Prince to carry the glass case back to his Palace, but going along a rough track, one of the dwarfs stumbled and the case was jolted. At once the piece of poisoned apple fell from Snow White's mouth.

She opened her eyes and, raising the lid of the glass case, she sat up and smiled at them all.

The Prince and the dwarfs were overjoyed to see her alive and well, and the Prince asked her to honour him by becoming his wife. Snow White consented because she loved the Prince on sight, and the Prince promised that the dwarfs would be looked after all their lives.

So everyone lived happily ever after—everyone, that is, but the wicked Queen who was banished from the king-dom for ever.

FAVOURITE VERSES
from Robert Louis Stevenson's
A CHILD'S GARDEN OF VERSES

Contents

PAGE

Bed in Summer   108
In winter I get up at night

At the Seaside   110
When I was down beside the sea

Autumn Fires   111
In the other gardens

Rain   112
The rain is raining all around

Foreign Lands   114
Up into the cherry-tree

The Land of Nod   116
From breakfast on through all the day

Where Go the Boats?   118
Dark brown is the river

The Cow   120
The friendly cow, all red and white

My Shadow   121
I have a little shadow that goes in and out with me

Escape at Bedtime   124
The lights from the parlour and kitchen shone out

Happy Thought   126
The world is so full of a number of things

The Wind   127
I saw you toss the kites on high

The Land of Counterpane   130
When I was sick and lay a-bed

The Swing   131
How do you like to go up in a swing

The Moon   132
The moon has a face like the clock in the hall

The Lamplighter   134
My tea is nearly ready and the sun has left the sky

Winter Time   136
Late lies the wintry sun a-bed

Farewell to the farm   138
The coach is at the door at last

The Dumb Soldier   140
When the grass was closely mown

Fairy Bread   143
Come up here, O dusty feet!

These illustrations first appeared in Hilda Boswell's
TREASURY—A CHILD'S GARDEN OF VERSES

BED
IN
SUMMER

IN winter I get up at night
And dress by yellow candle-light.
In summer, quite the other way,
I have to go to bed by day.

I have to go to bed and see
The birds still hopping on the tree,
Or hear the grown-up people's feet
Still going past me in the street.

And does it not seem hard to you,
When all the sky is clear and blue,
And I should like so much to play,
To have to go to bed by day?

AT THE SEASIDE

WHEN I was down beside the sea,
A wooden spade they gave to me
    To dig the sandy shore.
My holes were empty like a cup,
In every hole the sea came up
    Till it could come no more.

AUTUMN FIRES

IN the other gardens
    And all up the vale,
From the autumn bonfires
    See the smoke trail !

Pleasant summer over,
    And all the summer flowers,
The red fire blazes,
    The grey smoke towers.

Sing a song of seasons !
    Something bright in all !
Flowers in the summer,
    Fires in the fall !

RAIN

THE rain is raining all around,
  It falls on field and tree,
It rains on the umbrellas here,
  And on the ships at sea.

FOREIGN LANDS

Up into the cherry-tree
Who should climb but little me?
I held the trunk with both my hands
And looked abroad on foreign lands.

I saw the next-door garden lie,
Adorned with flowers, before my eye,
And many pleasant places more
That I had never seen before.

I saw the dimpling river pass
And be the sky's blue looking-glass;
The dusty roads go up and down
With people tramping into town.

If I could find a higher tree,
Farther and farther I should see,
To where the grown-up river slips
Into the sea among the ships.

To where the roads on either hand
Lead onward into fairy land,
Where all the children dine at five,
And all the playthings come alive.

THE LAND OF NOD

FROM breakfast on through all the day
At home among my friends I stay;
But every night I go abroad
Afar into the land of Nod.

All by myself I have to go,
With none to tell me what to do—
All alone beside the streams
And up the mountain-sides of dreams.

The strangest things are there for me,
Both things to eat and things to see,
And many frightening sights abroad
Till morning in the land of Nod.

Try as I like to find the way,
I never can get back by day,
Nor can remember plain and clear
The curious music that I hear.

WHERE GO
THE BOATS?

Dark brown is the river,
Golden is the sand.
It flows along for ever,
With trees on either hand.

Green leaves a-floating,
Castles of the foam,
Boats of mine a-boating—
Where will all come home?

On goes the river
　And out past the mill,
Away down the valley,
　Away down the hill.

　　Away down the river,
　　　A hundred miles or more,
　　Other little children
　　　Shall bring my boats ashore.

THE COW

THE friendly cow, all red and white,
 I love with all my heart :
She gives me cream with all her might,
 To eat with apple tart.

She wanders lowing here and there,
 And yet she cannot stray,
All in the pleasant open air,
 The pleasant light of day ;

And blown by all the winds that pass
 And wet with all the showers,
She walks among the meadow grass
 And eats the meadow flowers.

MY SHADOW

I HAVE a little shadow that goes in and out with me,
And what can be the use of him is more than I can
    see.
He is very, very like me from the heels up to the
    head ;
And I see him jump before me, when I jump into
    my bed.

The funniest thing about him is the way he likes
    to grow—
Not at all like proper children, which is always
    very slow;
For he sometimes shoots up taller like an india-
    rubber ball,
And he sometimes gets so little that there's none
    of him at all.

He hasn't got a notion of how children ought to
    play,
And can only make a fool of me in every sort of
    way.
He stays so close beside me, he's a coward you can
    see ;
I'd think shame to stick to nursie as that shadow
    sticks to me!

One morning, very early, before the sun was up,
I rose and found the shining dew on every butter-
    cup ;
But my lazy little shadow, like an arrant sleepy-
    head,
Had stayed at home behind me and was fast asleep
    in bed.

ESCAPE AT BEDTIME

THE lights from the parlour and kitchen shone out
   Through the blinds and the windows and bars ;
And high overhead and all moving about,
   There were thousands of millions of stars.
There ne'er were such thousands of leaves on a tree,
   Nor of people in church or the Park,
As the crowds of the stars that looked down upon
    me,
   And that glittered and winked in the dark.

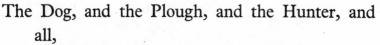

The Dog, and the Plough, and the Hunter, and
   all,
  And the star of the sailor, and Mars,
These shone in the sky, and the pail by the wall
  Would be half full of water and stars.

They saw me at last, and they chased me with
   cries,
  And they soon had me packed into bed ;
But the glory kept shining and bright in my eyes,
  And the stars going round in my head.

HAPPY THOUGHT

THE world is so full of a number of
   things,
I'm sure we should all be as happy as
   Kings.

THE WIND

I SAW you toss the kites on high
And blow the birds about the sky;
And all around I heard you pass,
Like ladies' skirts across the grass—
    O wind, a-blowing all day long,
    O wind, that sings so loud a song!

I saw the different things you did,
But always you yourself you hid.
I felt you push, I heard you call,
I could not see yourself at all—
    O wind, a-blowing all day long,
    O wind, that sings so loud a song!

O you that are so strong and cold,
O blower, are you young or old?
Are you a beast of field and tree,
Or just a stronger child than me?
O wind, a-blowing all day long,
O wind, that sings so loud a song!

THE LAND OF COUNTERPANE

WHEN I was sick and lay a-bed,
I had two pillows at my head,
And all my toys beside me lay
To keep me happy all the day.

And sometimes for an hour or so
I watched my leaden soldier go,
With different uniforms and drills,
Among the bed-clothes, through the hills ;

And sometimes sent my ships in fleets
All up and down among the sheets ;
Or brought my trees and houses out,
And planted cities all about.

I was the giant, great and still,
That sits upon the pillow-hill,
And sees before him, dale and plain,
The pleasant land of counterpane.

THE SWING

How do you like to go up in a swing,
  Up in the air so blue?
Oh, I do think it the pleasantest thing
  Ever a child can do!

Up in the air and over the wall,
  Till I can see so wide,
Rivers and trees and cattle and all
  Over the countryside—

Till I look down on the garden green,
  Down on the roof so brown—
Up in the air I go flying again,
  Up in the air and down!

THE MOON

THE moon has a face like the clock in the hall ;
She shines on thieves on the garden wall,
On streets and fields and harbour quays,
And birdies asleep in the forks of the trees.

The squalling cat and the squeaking mouse,
The howling dog by the door of the house,
The bat that lies in bed at noon,
All love to be out by the light of the moon.

But all of the things that belong to the day
Cuddle to sleep to be out of her way ;
And flowers and children close their eyes
Till up in the morning the sun shall rise.

133

THE LAMPLIGHTER

My tea is nearly ready and the sun has left the sky;
It's time to take the window to see Leerie going by;
For every night at tea-time and before you take
    your seat,
With lantern and with ladder he comes posting up
    the street.

Now Tom would be a driver and Maria go to sea,
And my papa's a banker and as rich as he can be;
But I, when I am stronger and can choose what I'm to do,
O Leerie, I'll go round at night and light the lamps with you!
For we are very lucky, with a lamp before the door,
And Leerie stops to light it as he lights so many more;
And O! before you hurry by with ladder and with light,
O Leerie, see a little child and nod to him to-night!

WINTER TIME

Late lies the wintry sun a-bed,
A frosty, fiery sleepy-head ;
Blinks but an hour or two ; and then,
A blood-red orange, sets again.

Before the stars have left the skies,
At morning in the dark I rise ;
And shivering in my nakedness,
By the cold candle, bathe and dress.

Close by the jolly fire I sit
To warm my frozen bones a bit ;
O with a reindeer-sled, explore
The colder countries round the door.

When, to go out, my nurse doth wrap
Me in my comforter and cap :
The cold wind burns my face, and blows
Its frosty pepper up my nose.

Black are my steps on silver sod ;
Thick blows my frosty breath abroad ;
And tree and house, and hill and lake,
Are frosted like a wedding-cake.

FAREWELL TO THE FARM

THE coach is at the door at last ;
The eager children, mounting fast
And kissing hands, in chorus sing :
Good-bye, good-bye, to everything !

To house and garden, field and lawn,
The meadow-gates we swang upon,
To pump and stable, tree and swing,
Good-bye, good-bye, to everything !

And fare you well for evermore,
O ladder at the hayloft door,
O hayloft where the cobwebs cling,
Good-bye, good-bye, to everything !

Crack goes the whip, and off we go ;
The trees and houses smaller grow ;
Last, round the woody turn we swing :
Good-bye, good-bye, to everything !

THE DUMB SOLDIER

WHEN the grass was closely mown,
Walking on the lawn alone,
In the turf a hole I found
And hid a soldier underground.

Spring and daisies came apace;
Grasses hide my hiding-place;
Grasses run like a green sea
O'er the lawn up to my knee.

Under grass alone he lies,
Looking up with leaden eyes,
Scarlet coat and pointed gun,
To the stars and to the sun.

When the grass is ripe like grain,
When the scythe is stoned again,
When the lawn is shaven clear,
Then my hole shall reappear.

I shall find him, never fear,
I shall find my grenadier ;
But, for all that's gone and come,
I shall find my soldier dumb.

He has lived, a little thing,
In the grassy woods of spring ;
Done, if he could tell me true,
Just as I should like to do.

He has seen the starry hours
And the springing of the flowers ;
And the fairy things that pass
In the forests of the grass.

In the silence he has heard
Talking bee and ladybird,
And the butterfly has flown
O'er him as he lay alone.

Not a word will he disclose,
Not a word of all he knows.
I must lay him on the shelf,
And make up the tale myself.

FAIRY BREAD

Come up here, O dusty feet!
Here is fairy bread to eat.
Here in my retiring room,
 Children, you may dine
On the golden smell of broom
 And the shade of pine;
And when you have eaten well,
Fairy stories hear and tell.

FAVOURITE STORIES

Contents

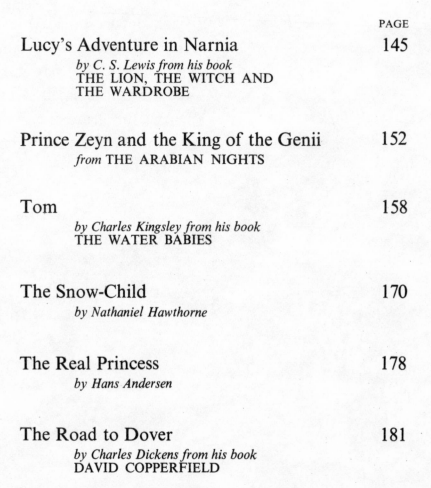

PAGE

Lucy's Adventure in Narnia   145
by C. S. Lewis from his book
THE LION, THE WITCH AND
THE WARDROBE

Prince Zeyn and the King of the Genii   152
from THE ARABIAN NIGHTS

Tom   158
by Charles Kingsley from his book
THE WATER BABIES

The Snow-Child   170
by Nathaniel Hawthorne

The Real Princess   178
by Hans Andersen

The Road to Dover   181
by Charles Dickens from his book
DAVID COPPERFIELD

These stories and pictures first appeared in
Hilda Boswell's TREASURY OF CHILDREN'S STORIES

Extract from *The Lion, the Witch and the Wardrobe* reprinted by
permission of *Geoffrey Bles Ltd.* and *The Macmillan Company, New York;*

LUCY'S ADVENTURE IN NARNIA

C. S. LEWIS

ONCE there were four children whose names were Peter, Susan, Edmund and Lucy. They were sent away from London during the war to the house of an old professor who lived in the heart of the country. It was the sort of house that you never seem to come to the end of, and it was full of unexpected places. One room was quite empty except for a big wardrobe.

"Nothing there!" said Peter as they explored the house. Lucy stayed behind because she thought it would be worth while trying the door of the wardrobe. To her surprise, it opened quite easily. She stepped inside among several long fur coats which were hanging there, for there was nothing she liked so much as the smell and feel of fur. Of course, she left the door open because she knew it was very foolish to shut oneself into any wardrobe. It was almost quite dark and she kept her arms stretched out in front of her so as not to bump her face into the back of the wardrobe.

"This must be a simply enormous wardrobe!" thought Lucy, going still further in. Then she noticed that there was something crunching under her feet. "I wonder is it moth-balls?" she thought, stooping down to feel it with her hands. But instead of feeling hard, smooth wood, she felt something soft and powdery and extremely cold. "This is very queer," she said.

Next moment she found that what was rubbing against her face and hands was no longer soft fur but something hard and rough and even prickly. "Why, it is just like branches of trees!" exclaimed Lucy. And then she saw that there was a light ahead of her; not a few inches away where the back of the wardrobe ought to have been, but a long way off. A moment later she found that she was standing in the middle of a wood at night-time with snow under her feet and snowflakes falling through the air.

Lucy felt a little frightened, but she felt very inquisitive and excited as well. She looked back over her shoulder and there, between the dark tree-trunks, she could still see the open doorway of the wardrobe. "I can always get back if anything goes wrong," thought Lucy.

In about ten minutes she reached the light and found it was a lamp-post. As she stood looking at it, wondering why there was a lamp-post in the middle of a wood, she heard a pitter patter of feet coming towards her. And soon after that a very strange person stepped out from among the trees. He was only a little taller than Lucy herself and he carried over his head an umbrella, white with snow. From the waist upwards he was like a man, but his legs were shaped like a goat's (the hair on them was glossy and black) and instead of feet he had goat's hoofs. He also had a tail, but Lucy did not notice this at first because it was neatly caught up over the arm that held the umbrella so as to keep it from trailing in the snow. He had a red woollen muffler round his neck and his skin was rather reddish too. He had a strange but pleasant little face, with a short pointed beard and curly hair, and out of the hair there stuck two horns, one on each side of his forehead. When he saw Lucy he gave a start of surprise.

"Goodness gracious me!" exclaimed the faun.

"Good evening," said Lucy. The faun made her a little bow.

"Good evening, good evening. Should I be right in thinking that you are a Daughter of Eve?"

"My name's Lucy," said she, not quite understanding him.

"But you are what they call a girl?" asked the faun.

"Of course I'm a girl," said Lucy.

"You are, in fact, human?"

"Of course I'm human," said Lucy.

"To be sure, to be sure," said the faun. "How stupid of me! But I've never seen a Son of Adam or a Daughter of Eve before. I am delighted. Allow me to introduce myself. My name is Tumnus. May I ask, O, Lucy Daughter of Eve, how you have come into Narnia?"

"Narnia?" said Lucy.

"This is the land of Narnia," said the faun. "Have you come from the wild woods of the west?"

"I—I got in through the wardrobe in the spare room," said Lucy.

"Ah!" said Mr. Tumnus, "if only I had worked harder at geography when I was a little faun, I should no doubt know all about those strange countries."

"But they aren't countries at all," said Lucy. "It's only just back there—at least—I'm not sure. It is summer there."

"Meanwhile," said Mr. Tumnus, "it is winter in Narnia, and has been for ever so long, and we shall both catch cold if we stand here talking in the snow. Daughter of Eve from the far land of Spare Oom where eternal summer reigns around the bright city of War Drobe, how would it be if you came and had tea with me?"

"Thank you very much, Mr. Tumnus," said Lucy. "But I was wondering whether I ought to be getting back."

"It's only just round the corner," said the faun, "and there'll be a roaring fire—and toast—and sardines—and cake."

"Well, it's very kind of you," said Lucy.

"If you will take my arm, Daughter of Eve," said Mr. Tumnus, "I shall be able to hold the umbrella over both of us."

And so Lucy found herself walking through the wood arm in arm with this strange creature as if they had known one another all their lives.

They had not gone far before they came to a place where the ground became rough. Mr. Tumnus turned suddenly aside as if he were going to walk straight into an unusually large rock, but at the last moment Lucy found he was leading her into the entrance of a cave. As soon as they were inside she found herself blinking in the light of a wood fire. Then Mr. Tumnus stooped and took a flaming piece of wood out of the fire with a neat little pair of tongs, and lit a lamp. "Now we shan't be long," he said, and immediately put a kettle on.

Lucy thought she had never been in a nicer place. It was a little dry, clean cave of reddish stone with a carpet on the floor and two little chairs and a table and a dresser and a mantelpiece over the fire and above that a picture of an old faun with a grey beard.

Mr. Tumnus set out the tea things. "Now, Daughter of Eve!" he said. And really it was a wonderful tea. There was a nice brown egg, lightly boiled, for each of them, and then sardines on toast, and then buttered toast, and then toast with honey, and then a sugar-topped cake. And when Lucy was tired of eating the faun began to talk. He had wonderful tales to tell of life in the forest. Then he took from its case on the dresser a strange little flute that looked as if it were made of straw, and began to play. And the tune he played made Lucy want to cry and laugh and dance and go to sleep all at the same time. It must have been hours later when she shook herself and said:

"Oh, Mr. Tumnus, I really must go home. I only meant to stay for a few minutes."

"It's no good *now*, you know," said the faun, laying down its flute and shaking its head at her very sorrowfully.

"No good?" said Lucy, jumping up. "What do you mean? I've got to go home at once. The others will be wondering what has happened to me." But a moment later she asked, "Mr. Tumnus! Whatever is the matter?" for the faun's brown eyes had filled with tears and then the tears began to trickle down its cheeks, and at last it covered its face with its hands and began to howl.

"Mr. Tumnus!" said Lucy in great distress. "Do tell me what is wrong." But the faun continued sobbing as if its heart would break. "Mr. Tumnus!" bawled Lucy in his ear. "Stop it at once! What on earth are you crying about?"

"Oh—oh—oh!" sobbed Mr. Tumnus, "I'm crying because I'm such a bad faun."

"I don't think you're a bad faun at all," said Lucy. "You are the nicest faun I've ever met."

"Oh—oh—you wouldn't say that if you knew," replied Mr. Tumnus between his sobs.

"But what have you done?" asked Lucy.

"Taken service under the White Witch. I'm in the pay of the White Witch. It is she that has got all Narnia under her thumb. It's she that makes it always winter. Always winter and never Christmas; think of that!"

"How awful!" said Lucy. "But what does she pay *you* for?"

"I'm a kidnapper for her, that's what I am," said Mr. Tumnus with a deep groan. "Look at me, Daughter of Eve. Would you believe that I'm the sort of faun to meet a poor innocent child in the wood, pretend to be friendly with it, and invite it home to my cave, all for the sake of lulling it asleep and then handing it over to the White Witch?"

"No," said Lucy. "I'm sure you wouldn't do anything of the sort."

"But I have," said the faun.

"Well," said Lucy slowly, "well, that was pretty bad. But you're so sorry for it that I'm sure you will never do it again."

"Daughter of Eve, don't you understand?" said the faun. "I'm doing it now."

"What do you mean?" cried Lucy, turning very white.

"You are the child," said Tumnus. "I had orders from the White Witch that if ever I saw a Son of Adam or a Daughter of Eve in the wood, I was to catch them and hand them over to her. And you are the first I ever met."

"Oh, but you won't, Mr. Tumnus," said Lucy. "You won't, will you?"

"If I don't," said he, beginning to cry again, "she's sure to find out. She'll turn me into stone and I shall be only a statue of a faun."

"I'm very sorry, Mr. Tumnus," said Lucy. "But please let me go home."

"Of course I will," said the faun. "I hadn't known what humans were like before I met you. We must go as quietly as we can. The whole wood is full of *her* spies."

The journey back was not at all like the journey to the faun's cave; they stole along as quickly as they could, without speaking a word, and Mr. Tumnus kept to the darkest places. Lucy was relieved when they reached the lamp-post again.

She looked very hard between the trees and could just see in the distance a patch of light that looked like daylight. "I can see the wardrobe door," she said.

"Farewell, Daughter of Eve," said the faun. "C-can you ever forgive me?"

"Why, of course I can," said Lucy. "And I do hope you won't get into dreadful trouble on my account," and she ran towards the far-off patch of daylight as quickly as her legs would carry her.

Presently, instead of rough branches brushing past her she felt coats, and instead of crunching snow under her feet she felt wooden boards, and all at once she found herself jumping out of the wardrobe into the same empty room from which the adventure had started. She shut the wardrobe door tightly behind her. She could hear the voices of the others in the passage.

"I'm here," she shouted. "I've come back. I'm all right!"

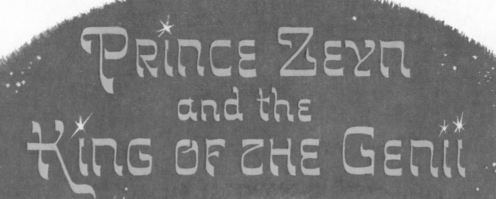

Prince Zeyn and the King of the Genii

A story from The Arabian Nights.

THERE was once a King of Balsora who was very rich and good, and much loved by all the people whom he ruled. He had one son, whose name was Zeyn. Gathering together all the wise men in his country, he asked them to find out what sort of a boy the young Prince would be. So the wise men went out into the palace garden on a fine starlit night, and, looking up at the stars, said they could see wonderful things that would happen to Prince Zeyn.

"The stars say he will be very brave," said one wise man.

"They tell me that he will have strange adventures," said another.

"And he will live to be very old," added a third.

The young Prince grew up, and was taught everything that princes ought to know; but when he was still quite young, his father was taken very ill. Knowing that he was going to die, he sent for Prince Zeyn.

"You will soon be the king of this country," he said. "And I hope you will be a good one. Do not listen to those who are always praising you, and try to find out the real truth before you punish any one."

Prince Zeyn promised to remember his father's words, and afterwards the old king died.

At first Zeyn was not a good king. Being able to do whatever he liked, he spent most of his time in amusing himself and spending money. His mother, a very wise queen, reminded him of his father's words, and he began to feel sorry that he was not a better king, whom his people could love as they had loved his father.

But his money was all spent, and, not knowing where to get any more, he felt sad. One night he had a wonderful dream. He looked up and saw an old man standing beside his bed and smiling kindly down upon him.

"Oh, Zeyn," said the old man, "joy comes after sorrow, and happiness after sadness. The time of your riches has come. Tomorrow morning, take an axe, and dig in your father's room. There you will find a great treasure."

Now Zeyn did not believe this, but, feeling rather curious, he told the Queen his dream, and then, sending for an axe, shut himself up alone in his father's room. He dug up the pavement until he was quite tired, but at last his axe struck against a white stone, which he lifted eagerly.

To his surprise, he found a door fastened with a padlock. The axe soon broke this, and there, before the Prince, a marble staircase went down into the earth. Lighting a taper, Zeyn ran down, to find himself in a fine chamber with a crystal floor. All round it were shelves, and on the shelves ten big urns.

Zeyn took off the lid of the first urn, and found it full of gold. He then looked into the other urns, and behold, every one was full of gold. He took a handful to the Queen, who was greatly astonished, and went with him to the room where the treasure was hidden.

In one corner the Queen saw another little urn, and inside it was nothing but a key. "This must lead to another treasure," they said, and, looking round the room, found a lock in the middle of the wall, which the key just fitted. When it was turned, this door opened, and showed a large hall in which stood eight shining diamond statues upon eight large gold pedestals.

But there was one more pedestal which had no statue, and above it lay a piece of white satin on which Zeyn read these words written by his father: *My dear son, all these statues are for you. Go to Cairo and find an old slave of mine called Mobarec. He will show you a place where you may find a ninth statue more beautiful than all the rest.*

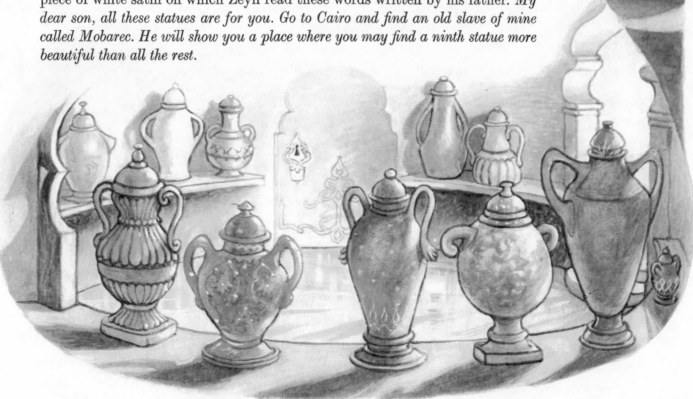

When he had read this, Zeyn set off to discover the ninth statue to fill the empty pedestal. Going to Cairo, he soon found the old slave Mobarec, who was now one of the richest men in the city.

"I am the son of the King of Balsora," said Zeyn.

"And how shall I know that you are speaking the truth?" said the old slave, looking straight into Zeyn's eyes.

"Because I can tell you my father had a secret room in which were ten urns full of gold and eight diamond statues. I have come to you to ask you where to find the ninth."

"You are indeed the young Prince!" cried Mobarec.

The next morning, Zeyn and Mobarec set out on their search for the ninth statue. The old man said that the Prince must be prepared to face many dangers, but as Zeyn was longing for adventures this did not frighten him.

After travelling for many days they came to some tall and waving palm trees, standing all around a lake of shining water. A silver moon looked through the trees and everything was very silent.

"You will now need all your courage," whispered Mobarec. "We are near the dreadful place where the ninth statue is guarded. We shall have to cross this water."

"But we have no boat," answered Zeyn.

"Wait a moment," said Mobarec, "and a fairy boat belonging to the King of the Genii will appear. But, however strange it looks, be very careful not to make a sound. If you speak, we shall all go to the bottom and be drowned."

Mobarec shaded his eyes and looked across the shining water. A little boat came into sight with an amber mast and a floating sail of blue satin. In a moment they had crossed the lake, the only sound being the soft rush of oars in the water.

"We may speak now," said Mobarec. "We are on a beautiful island belonging to the King of the Genii."

Very soon they came in front of an emerald castle with a golden gate, where several tall genii stood as guards. They were the fairies who lived on the island, and were tall and terrible to look at to those who did not understand them. But Mobarec did; so he took from under his robe two little square carpets, one for Zeyn, and one for himself. These were magic carpets, and those who sat on them were quite safe.

"The King of the Genii will be here soon now," said Mobarec. "If he is angry with us for coming, he will look like a monster; but if he is pleased, he will be very handsome."

There was a flash of lightning, a loud noise of thunder, and then all the island went dark. Suddenly a big, fine-looking man stood before them, and began to smile.

"Welcome, Prince Zeyn," he said. "I loved your father, and whenever he came to see me, I gave him a diamond statue for his very own. It was I whom you saw in your dreams, and I promised your father to give you the ninth statue, which is the most beautiful of all.

"But there is only one way to get it. You must search the world until you find a beautiful maiden who is not only clever but who has never in her life spoken an angry word or thought a wicked thought. When you have found her, bring her back here, to wait upon my Queen, and then I will give you the statue."

Zeyn promised to do all this, though he knew it would be a hard task; but he asked the King of the Genii how he should know the maiden.

"Here is a magic mirror," replied the King. "Only the right maiden will be able to see her face in this."

So Mobarec and Prince Zeyn went away into the world again to find a perfect maiden. They gathered together all the beautiful girls in Cairo, but not one of them could see her own face in the mirror. It grew dark and clouded whenever they looked into it. They next went to Baghdad, where they made friends with an old man named Muezin, who told them that he knew the most perfect maiden in the world.

She lived with her father, who had once been a great man at the King's court, but who now spent all his time teaching his daughter to be clever and good. Muezin took Prince Zeyn to see her, and when her father heard that he was the son of the King of Balsora, he was very pleased to see him, and at once allowed his daughter to look into the magic mirror.

The moment she did so, she saw her own lovely face in the shining glass, and every one standing round saw it too. Zeyn had found the perfect maiden that he sought. Now there was only one way for him to get the maiden, and that was to marry her. Zeyn was quite ready to do this, for she was so good and beautiful that he already loved her. Indeed, he found it very hard to keep his promise, and take her back to the King of the Genii. He thought he would rather have the perfect maiden than the ninth statue.

The King of the magic island was very pleased with the maiden, and said she would be a beautiful slave for his Queen. Then he turned to Prince Zeyn and said, "I am quite satisfied with all you have done. Go home now, and when you reach your palace at Balsora, go down at once into the room where the eight diamond statues are. There you will find the ninth statue, standing on its pedestal."

Prince Zeyn went sadly home with Mobarec, leaving his lovely bride behind him. As soon as he reached the palace he told his mother all that had happened, and she was delighted to hear he would so soon have the ninth statue.

"Come, my son," she said, "let us both go down and look for the new treasure."

Together they went through the stone door, and down the marble staircase. They came to the diamond statues, and there Prince Zeyn stood still in surprise and delight. For the ninth statue was not made of diamonds or gold; it was the beautiful and perfect maiden whom he loved and whom he had been so sad to leave.

TOM

CHARLES KINGSLEY

ONCE upon a time there was a little chimney-sweep, and his name was Tom.

Now I dare say you never got up at three o'clock on a midsummer morning. Some people get up then because they want to catch salmon; and some, because they want to climb the Alps; and a great many more, because they must, like Tom.

One day a smart little groom rode into the court where Tom lived and halloed to him to know where Mr. Grimes, the chimney-sweep, lived. Mr. Grimes was to come up next morning to Sir John Harthover's at the Place, for his old chimney-sweep was gone to prison, and the chimneys wanted sweeping.

So Tom and his master set out; Grimes rode the donkey in front, and Tom and the brushes walked behind; out of the court, and up the street, past the closed window shutters, and the winking weary policemen, and the roofs all shining grey in the grey dawn. On they went; and Tom looked, and looked, for he never had been so far into the country before.

Soon they came up with a poor Irishwoman, trudging along with a bundle at her back. She had neither shoes nor stockings, and limped along as if she were tired and footsore. Mr. Grimes called out to her.

"This is a hard road. Will ye up and ride behind me?"

But she answered quietly: "No thank you; I'd sooner walk with your little lad here."

So she walked beside Tom and talked to him and asked him where he lived, and what he knew, and all about himself, till Tom thought he had never met such a pleasant-spoken woman. Then he asked her where she lived; and she said far away by the sea. And Tom asked her about the sea; and she told him how it rolled and roared over the rocks in winter nights, and lay still in the bright summer days, for the children to bathe and play in it; and many a story more, till Tom longed to go and see the sea, and bathe in it likewise.

At last, at the bottom of a hill, they came to a spring and there Grimes stopped. Without a word, he got off his donkey, and clambered over the low wall, and knelt down, and began dipping his ugly head into the spring.

"I wish I might go and dip my head in," said poor little Tom.

"Thou come along," said Grimes, "what dost want with washing thyself?" Grimes was very sulky, because the woman preferred Tom's company to his; so he dashed at Tom and began beating him.

"Are you not ashamed of yourself, Thomas Grimes?" cried the Irishwoman over the wall.

Grimes looked up, startled at her knowing his name; but all he answered was, "No: nor never was yet;" and went on beating Tom.

"Stop!" said the Irishwoman. "If you strike that boy again, I can tell what I know. I have one more word for you both.

Those that wish to be clean,
Clean they will be;
And those that wish to be foul,
Foul they will be.

Remember."

And she turned away and through a gate into the meadow. Grimes rushed after her, shouting, "You come back!" But when he got into the meadow the woman was not there. There was no place to hide in, but look where he would, she was not there.

They had gone three miles and more, and came to Sir John's lodge-gates. Grimes rang at the gate, and out came a keeper on the spot and opened. They walked up a great lime avenue, a full mile long, and between their stems Tom peeped trembling at the horns of the sleeping deer, which stood up among the ferns. Tom had never seen such enormous trees, and as he looked up he fancied that the blue sky rested on their heads.

"I wish I were a keeper," said Tom, "to live in such a beautiful place, and wear green velveteens and have a real dog-whistle at my button, like you."

The keeper laughed; he was a kind-hearted fellow.

By this time they were come up to the great iron gates in front of the house; and Tom stared through them at the house itself, and wondered how many chimneys there were in it.

But Tom and his master did not go in through the great iron gates, as if they had been Dukes or Bishops, but round the back way, and a very long way round it was; and into a little back door, where the ash-boy let them in, yawning horribly; and then in a passage the housekeeper met them, and she gave Grimes solemn orders about, "You will take care of this, and take care of that."

And Grimes listened, and said every now and then, under his voice, "You'll mind that, you little beggar?" and Tom did mind, all at least that he could. And then the housekeeper turned them into a grand room, all covered up in sheets of brown paper, and bade them begin in a lofty and tremendous voice; and so, after a whimper or two, and a kick from his master, into the grate Tom went, and up the chimney.

How many chimneys he swept I cannot say; but he swept so many that he got quite tired, and puzzled too, for they were not like the town flues to which he was accustomed, but such as you would find—if you would only get up them and look, which perhaps you would not like to do—in old country houses; large and crooked chimneys, which had been altered again and again, till they ran into one another. So Tom fairly lost his way in them; not that he cared much for that, though he was in pitchy darkness, for he was as much at home in a chimney as a mole is underground; but at last, coming down, as he thought, the right chimney, he came down the wrong one, and found himself standing on the hearthrug in a room the like of which he had never seen before.

The room was all dressed in white; white window curtains, white bed curtains, white furniture, and white walls, with just a few lines of pink here and there. The carpet was all over gay little flowers; and the walls were hung with pictures in gilt frames. There were pictures of ladies and gentlemen and pictures of horses and dogs.

The next thing he saw, and that puzzled him, was a washing-stand, with ewers and basins, and soap and brushes, and towels; and a large bath, full of clean water—what a heap of things all for washing! "She must be a very dirty lady," thought Tom, "to want as much scrubbing as all that."

And then, looking towards the bed, he saw that dirty lady, and held his breath with astonishment. Under the snow-white coverlet, upon the snow-white pillow, lay the most beautiful little girl that Tom had ever seen. Her cheeks were almost as white as the pillow, and her hair was like threads of gold spread all about over the bed. She might have been as old as Tom, or maybe a year or two older; but Tom did not think of that. He thought only of her delicate skin and golden hair, and wondered whether she were a real live person, or one of the wax dolls he had seen in the shops. But when he saw her breathe, he made up his mind that she was alive, and stood staring at her, as if she had been an angel out of heaven.

And then he thought, "And are all people like that when they are washed?"
And he looked at his own wrist, and tried to rub the soot off, and wondered
whether it ever would come off. And looking round he suddenly saw, standing
close to him, a little ugly, black, ragged figure, with bleared eyes and grinning
white teeth. He turned on it angrily. What did such a little black ape want in
that sweet young lady's room? And behold, it was himself, reflected in a
great mirror, the like of which Tom had never seen before.

And Tom, for the first time in his life, found out that he was dirty; and
burst into tears with shame and anger; and turned to sneak up the chimney
again and hide, and upset the fender, and threw the fire-irons down, with a
noise as of ten thousand tin kettles tied to ten thousand mad dogs' tails.

Up jumped the little white lady in her bed, and, seeing Tom, screamed as
shrill as any peacock. In rushed a stout old nurse from the next room, and seeing
Tom, likewise made up her mind that he had come to rob, plunder, destroy,
and burn; and dashed at him as he lay over the fender, so fast that she caught
him by the jacket. But she did not hold him. Tom had been in a policeman's
hands many a time, and out of them too, what is more; so he doubled under
the good lady's arm, across the room, and out of the window in a moment.

But all under the window spread a tree, and down the tree he went, like a cat, and across the garden lawn, and over the iron railings, and up the park towards the wood, leaving the old nurse to scream murder and fire at the window.

The under gardener, mowing, saw Tom and threw down his scythe; and gave chase to poor Tom. The dairy-maid heard the noise, and gave chase to Tom. A groom, cleaning Sir John's hack at the stables, gave chase to Tom. Grimes ran out and gave chase to Tom. The old steward opened the park gate and gave chase to Tom. The ploughman left his horses and gave chase to Tom. The keeper ran after Tom. Sir John looked out of his study window, and up at the nurse, and he ran out and gave chase to Tom. The Irishwoman, too, was walking up to the house to beg; but she threw away her bundle and gave chase to Tom likewise. All ran up the park, shouting, "Stop thief!"

Tom, of course, made for the wood. He was sharp enough to know that he might hide in a bush, or swarm up a tree, and altogether, had more chance there than in the open. But when he got into the wood, the boughs laid hold of his legs and arms, the hassock-grass and sedges tumbled him over and the birches birched him.

"I must get out of this," thought Tom. And indeed I don't think he would ever have got out at all if he had not suddenly run his head against a wall. He guessed that over the wall the cover would end; and up it he went, and over like a squirrel. And there he was, out on the great grouse-moors, heather and bog and rock, stretching away and up, up to the very sky.

At last he came to a dip in the land, and went to the bottom of it, and then he turned bravely away from the wall and up the moor; for he knew that he had put a hill between him and his enemies, and could go on without their seeing him. But the Irishwoman, alone of them all, had seen which way Tom went.

So Tom went on, and on, he hardly knew why. What would Tom have said, if he had seen, walking over the moor behind him, the very same Irishwoman who had taken his part upon the road?

And now he began to get a little hungry, and very thirsty; but he could see nothing to eat anywhere, and still less to drink.

To his right rose moor after moor, hill after hill, till they faded away, blue into blue sky. But between him and those moors, and really at his very feet, lay something, to which, as soon as Tom saw it, he determined to go, for that was the place for him.

A deep, deep green and rocky valley, very narrow, and filled with wood; but through the wood, hundreds of feet below him, he could see a clear stream glance. Oh, if he could but get down to that stream! Then, by the stream, he saw the roof of a little cottage, and a little garden, set out in squares and beds. And there was a tiny little red thing moving in the garden, no bigger than a fly. As Tom looked down, he saw that it was a woman in a red petticoat! Ah! perhaps she would give him something to eat; and he could get down there in five minutes.

But Tom was wrong about getting down in five minutes, for the cottage was more than a mile off, and a good thousand feet below. However, down he went, though he was very footsore, and tired, and hungry, and thirsty, and all the while he never saw the Irishwoman going down behind him. At last he got to the bottom, and stumbled away, down over a low wall, and into a narrow road, and up to the cottage door. And a neat pretty cottage it was, with clipped yew hedges all round the garden, and yews inside too, cut into peacocks and trumpets and teapots and all kinds of queer shapes. He came slowly up to the open door, which was all hung round with clematis and roses; and then peeped in, half afraid.

And there sat by the empty fire-place, which was filled with a pot of sweet herbs, the nicest old woman that ever was seen, in her red petticoat, and short dimity bedgown, and clean white cap, with a black silk handkerchief over it, tied under her chin.

Such a pleasant cottage it was, with a shiny clean stone floor, and curious old prints on the wall, and an old black oak sideboard full of bright pewter and brass dishes, and a cuckoo clock in the corner, which began shouting as soon as Tom appeared: not that it was frightened at Tom, but that it was just eleven o'clock.

"What are thou, and what dost want?" cried the old dame. "A chimney-sweep! Away with thee. I'll have no sweeps here."

"Water," said poor little Tom, quite faint.

The old dame looked at him through her spectacles one minute and two, and three; and then she said: "He's sick; and a bairn's a bairn, sweep or none."

"Water," said Tom.

"God forgive me!" and she put by her spectacles, and rose, and came to Tom. "Water's bad for thee; I'll give thee milk."

Tom drank the milk off at one draught.

"Bless thy pretty heart! Come wi' me, and I'll hap thee up somewhere."

She put him in an outhouse upon soft sweet hay and an old rug, and bade him sleep. But Tom did not fall asleep. Instead of it he turned and tossed and kicked about in the strangest way, and felt so hot all over that he longed to get into the river and cool himself; and then he fell half asleep, and dreamt that he heard the little white lady crying to him, "Oh, you're so dirty; go and be washed;" and then that he heard the Irishwoman saying, "Those that wish to be clean, clean they will be." And he said out aloud again, though being half asleep he did not know it, "I must be clean, I must be clean."

And all of a sudden he found himself, not in the outhouse on the hay, but in the middle of a meadow, over the road, with a stream just before him, saying continually, "I must be clean, I must be clean." He had got there on his own legs, between sleep and awake, as children will often get out of bed, and go about the room, when they are not quite well. But he was not a bit surprised, and went on to the bank of the brook, and lay down on the grass, and looked into the clear, clear limestone water, with every pebble at the bottom bright and clean, while the little silver trout dashed about in fright at the sight of his black face; and he dipped his hand in and found it so cool, cool, cool; and he said, "I will be a fish; I will swim in the water; I must be clean, I must be clean."

So he pulled off all his clothes in such haste that he tore some of them, which was easy enough with such ragged old things. And he put his poor, hot, sore feet into the water; and then his legs. He was so hot and thirsty, and longed so to be clean for once, that he tumbled himself as quick as he could into the clear cool stream.

And he had not been in it two minutes before he fell fast asleep, into the quietest, sunniest, cosiest sleep that ever he had in his life; and he dreamt about the green meadows by which he had walked that morning, and the tall elm trees, and the sleeping cows; and after that he dreamt of nothing at all. The reason of his falling into such a delightful sleep is very simple. It was merely that the fairies took him.

And now comes the most wonderful part of this wonderful story. Tom, when he woke, for, of course, he woke, found himself swimming about in the stream, being about four inches long, and having a set of gills which he mistook for a lace frill, till he pulled at them, found he hurt himself, and made up his mind that they were part of himself and best left alone. In fact the fairies had turned him into a water baby.

A water baby? You never heard of a water baby? Perhaps not. That is the very reason why this story was written. There are a great many things in the world which you never heard of; and a great many more which nobody ever heard of; and a great many things too, which nobody will ever hear of.

But at all events, so it happened to Tom. And, therefore, the keeper, and the groom, and Sir John, made a great mistake, and were very unhappy (Sir John at least) without any reason, when they found a black thing in the water, and said it was Tom and that he had been drowned. They were utterly mistaken. Tom was quite alive; and cleaner, and merrier, than he ever had been. The fairies had washed him, you see, in the swift river, so thoroughly that not only his dirt, but his whole husk and shell had been washed quite off him, and the pretty little real Tom was washed out of the inside of it, and swam away.

But good Sir John did not understand all this, and he took it into his head that Tom was drowned. And all the while Tom was swimming about in the river, with a pretty little lace-collar of gills about his neck, as lively as a grig, and as clean as a fresh-run salmon.

The SNOW-CHILD

NATHANIEL HAWTHORNE

ONE afternoon of a cold winter's day, when the sun shone with chilly brightness after a long storm, two children asked leave of their mother to run out and play in the new-fallen snow. The elder child was a little girl called Violet, and her brother was known as Peony, on account of the ruddiness of his round little face. The children lived in a city, and had no wider play-place than a little garden in front of the house, divided by a white fence from the street, and with a pear-tree and two or three plum-trees overshadowing it, and some rose-bushes just in front of the parlour windows. The trees and shrubs, however, were now leafless, and their twigs were enveloped in the light snow.

"Yes, Violet. Yes, Peony," said their mother; "you may go out and play in the new snow."

Out went the two children, with a hop-skip-and-jump that carried them at once into the heart of a huge snowdrift. At last, when they had frosted one another all over with handfuls of snow, Violet was struck with a new idea.

"Peony," said she. "Let's make a figure out of snow—a little snow-girl—and it shall be our sister, and shall run about and play with us all winter. Won't it be nice?"

"Oh, yes!" cried Peony, as plainly as he could speak, for he was a very little boy. "That will be nice!"

"Yes," answered Violet; "Mamma shall see the new little girl. But she must not make her come into the warm parlour; for, you know, our little snow-sister will not like the warmth."

And at once the children began this great business of making a snow-child that should run about. Violet told Peony what to do, while she shaped out all the nicer parts of the snow-figure. It seemed, in fact, not so much to be made by the children, as to grow up under their hands.

"Oh, Violet, how beau-ti-ful she looks!" exclaimed Peony.

"Yes," said Violet. "I did not know, Peony, that we could make such a sweet little girl as this. Now bring me those light wreaths of snow from the lower branches of the pear-tree. I must have them to make our snow-sister's hair."

"Here they are!" answered the little boy. "Take care you do not break them."

"Now," said Violet in a very satisfied voice, "we must have some little shining bits of ice to make the brightness of her eyes."

"Let us call Mamma to look out," said Peony; and then he shouted loudly: "Mamma! Mamma! Mamma!!! Look out and see what a nice little girl we are making!"

The mother put down her work for an instant, and looked out of the window. Through the bright, blinding dazzle of the sun and the snow, she saw the two children at work. Indistinctly, she saw the snow-child, and thought to herself that never before was there a snow-figure so cleverly made. She sat down again to her work, and the children, too, kept busily at work in the garden.

"What a nice playmate she will be for us all winter long!" said Violet. "I hope Papa will not be afraid of her giving us a cold! Shan't you love her very much, Peony?"

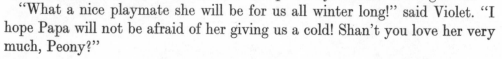

"Oh, yes!" cried Peony. "And I will hug her, and she shall sit down close by me, and drink some of my warm milk!"

"Oh, no, Peony!" answered Violet "That will not do at all. Warm milk will not be good for our little snow-sister. Little snow-people like her eat nothing but icicles."

There was a minute or two of silence; then, all of a sudden, Violet cried out:

"Look, Peony! A light has been shining on her cheek out of that rose-coloured cloud! And the colour does not go away! Isn't that beautiful?"

"Yes; it is beau-ti-ful," answered Peony. "Oh, Violet, look at her hair! It is all like gold!"

"Oh, yes," said Violet. "That colour, you know, comes from the golden clouds that we see up there in the sky."

Just then there came a breeze of the purest west wind, sweeping through the garden and rattling the parlour windows. It sounded so wintry cold, that the mother was about to tap on the window-pane with her thimbled finger to bring the two children in, when they both cried out to her.

"Mamma! Mamma! We have finished our little snow-sister, and she is running about the garden with us! Please look out and see."

The sun had now gone out of the sky and there was not the slightest gleam or dazzle, so that the mother could look all over the garden and see everything and everybody in it. Besides Violet and Peony, there was a small figure of a girl, dressed all in white, with rose-tinged cheeks and ringlets of golden hue, playing about the garden with the two children! The mother thought to herself that it must certainly be the daughter of one of the neighbours, and that, seeing Violet and Peony in the garden, the child had run across the street to play with them. So she went to the door, intending to invite the little runaway into her comfortable parlour. But, after opening the house door, she stood an instant on the threshold, hesitating. Indeed, she almost doubted whether it were a real child, after all, or only a light wreath of the new-fallen snow, blown hither and thither about the garden by the intensely cold west wind. Among all the children of the neighbourhood, the lady could remember no such face, with its pure white and delicate rose-colour. And as for her dress, which was entirely of white and fluttering in the breeze, it was such as no reasonable woman would put on a little girl when sending her out to play in the depth of winter. It made this kind and careful mother shiver only to look at those small feet, with nothing in the world on them except a very thin pair of white slippers. Nevertheless, the child seemed not to feel the cold but danced so lightly over the snow that the tips of her toes left hardly a print on its surface.

Once, in the course of their play, the strange child put herself between Violet and Peony, and took a hand of each; but Peony pulled away his little fist and began to rub it as if the fingers were tingling with cold; while Violet remarked that it was better not to take hold of hands. All this time the mother stood on the threshold, wondering how a little girl could look so much like a flying snowdrift, or how a snowdrift could look so very like a little girl.

She called Violet to her and whispered:

"Violet, my dear, what is this child's name? Does she live near us?"

"Why, Mamma," answered Violet, laughing, "this is our little snow-sister whom we have just been making!"

At this instant a flock of snow-birds came flitting through the air. They flew at once to the snow-child, fluttered eagerly about her head and alighted on her shoulders. She was as glad to see these little birds as they were to see her, and welcomed them by holding out both her hands.

"Violet," said her mother, greatly perplexed, "tell me the truth. Who is this little girl?"

"Mamma," answered Violet, looking into her mother's face, and surprised that she should need any further explanation, "I have told you truly who she is. It is our little snow-figure which Peony and I have been making."

While Mamma still hesitated what to think and what to do, the street-gate was thrown open and the father of Violet and Peony appeared, a fur cap drawn down over his ears and the thickest of gloves on his hands. His eyes brightened at the sight of his wife and children, although he could not help uttering a word or two of surprise at finding the whole family in the open air on so bleak a day, and after sunset too. He soon perceived the little white stranger, and the flock of snow-birds fluttering above her head.

"What little girl is this?" he inquired. "Surely her mother must be crazy to let her go out in such bitter weather with only that flimsy white dress and those thin slippers!"

"My dear," said his wife, "I know no more about the little thing than you do. Some neighbour's child, I suppose. Our Violet and Peony," she added, "insist that she is nothing but a snow-figure which they have been busy making in the garden almost all the afternoon."

As she said that, the mother glanced towards the spot where the children's snow-figure had been made. What was her surprise to see not the slightest trace of so much labour! No piled-up heap of snow! Only the prints of little footsteps around an empty space!

"This is very strange!" said she.

"What is strange?" asked Violet. "Father, do you not see how it is? This is our snow-figure which Peony and I have made because we wanted another playmate."

"Pooh, nonsense, child!" cried their father. "Do not tell me of making live figures out of snow. Come, wife; this little stranger must not stay out in the cold a moment longer. We will bring her into the parlour; and you shall give her a supper of warm bread and milk, and make her as comfortable as you can. Meanwhile I will inquire among the neighbours; or, if necessary, send the city-crier about the streets to give notice of a lost child."

"Father," cried Violet, putting herself before him, "it is true what I have been telling you! This is our little snow-girl, and she cannot live unless she breathes the cold west wind. Do not make her come into the hot room!"

"Nonsense, child, nonsense, nonsense!" cried the father. "Run into the house this moment! It is too late to play any longer. I must take care of this little girl immediately, or she will catch her death of cold!"

The little white creature fled backwards, shaking her head as if to say, "Please do not touch me!"

Some of the neighbours, seeing him from their windows, wondered what could possess the poor man to be running about his garden in pursuit of a snowdrift. At length, he chased the little stranger into a corner where she could not possibly escape him. His wife had been looking on, and, it being nearly twilight, was wonder-struck to observe how the snow-child gleamed and sparkled, and when driven into the cor- ner, she positively glistened like a star!

"Come, you odd little thing!" cried the children's father, seizing her by the hand, and with a smile, he led the snow-child towards the house. As she followed him, all the glow and sparkle went out of her figure and she looked as dull and drooping as a thaw.

Violet and Peony, their eyes full of tears, entreated him not to bring their snow-sister into the house.

"Not bring her in!" exclaimed the kind-hearted man. "Why she is so cold, already, that her hand has almost frozen mine, in spite of my thick gloves. Would you have her freeze to death?"

The little white figure was led—drooping more and more—out of the frosty air, and into the comfortable parlour. A stove, filled to the brim with intensely burning coal, was sending a bright gleam through the glass of its iron door. The parlour was hung with red curtains and covered with a red carpet, and looked just as warm as it felt.

The father placed the snow-child on the hearth-rug, right in front of the hissing and fuming stove.

"Now she will be comfortable!" he cried, rubbing his hands and looking about him with the pleasantest smile you ever saw.

Sad, sad and drooping, looked the little white maiden as she stood on the hearth-rug with the hot blast of the stove striking through her. Once she threw a glance towards the windows and caught a glimpse of the snow-covered roofs, and the stars glimmering frostily.

"Come, wife, give her some warm supper as soon as the milk boils," said the good man and turning the collar of his coat up over his ears, he went out of the house, and had barely reached the street-gate when he was recalled by the screams of Violet and Peony.

"Husband! Husband!" cried his wife. "There is no need of going for the child's parents."

"We told you so, Father!" screamed Violet and Peony, as he re-entered the parlour. "You *would* bring her in; and now our poor—dear—little snow-sister is thawed!"

In the utmost perplexity, he demanded an explanation of his wife. She could only reply, that, being brought to the parlour by the cries of Violet and Peony, she found no trace of the little white maiden, except a heap of snow, which, while she was gazing at it, melted quite away upon the hearth-rug.

"And there you see all that is left of it!" added she, pointing to a pool of water in front of the stove.

"Yes, Father," said Violet, looking reproachfully at him through her tears, "there is all that is left of our dear little snow-sister!"

"Naughty Father!" cried Peony.

But there is no teaching anything to sensible men like Violet and Peony's father. They know everything that has been, and everything that is, and everything that possibly can be, and they will not recognise a miracle even if it come to pass under their very noses.

"Wife," said the children's father, after being silent for a time, "see what a quantity of snow the children have brought in on their feet! It has made quite a puddle here before the stove. Tell Dora to bring some towels and mop it up!"

THE REAL PRINCESS

HANS ANDERSEN

THERE was once a Prince who wished to marry a Princess; but, he said, she must be a *real* Princess. He travelled all over the world in hopes of finding such a lady; but there was always something wrong. Princesses he found in plenty; but whether they were real Princesses it was impossible for him to decide, for now one thing, now another, seemed to him not quite right about the ladies. At last he returned to his palace quite cast down, because he wished so much to have a real Princess for his wife.

One evening a fearful tempest arose. It thundered and lightened, and the rain poured down from the sky in torrents; besides, it was as dark as pitch. All at once there was heard a violent knocking at the door, and the old King, the Prince's father, went out himself to open it.

It was a Princess who was standing outside the door. What with the rain and the wind, she was in a sad condition. The water trickled down from her hair, and her clothes clung to her body. She said she was a real Princess.

"Ah, we shall soon see that!" thought the old Queen-mother. However, she said not a word of what she was going to do; but went quietly into the bedroom, took all the bed-clothes off the bed, and put three little peas on the bedstead. She then laid twenty mattresses one upon another over the three peas, and put twenty feather beds over the mattresses.

Upon this the princess was to pass the night.

The next morning she was asked how she had slept. "Oh, very badly indeed!" she replied. "I have scarcely closed my eyes the whole night through. I do not know what was in my bed, but I had something hard under me, and am all over black and blue. It has hurt me so much!"

Now it was plain that the lady must be a real Princess, since she had been able to feel the three little peas through the twenty mattresses and twenty feather beds. None but a real Princess could have had such a delicate sense of feeling.

The Prince accordingly made her his wife; being now convinced that he had found a real Princess. The three peas were, however, put into the cabinet of curiosities, where they are still to be seen, provided they are not lost.

Was not this a lady of real delicacy?

THE ROAD TO DOVER

CHARLES DICKENS

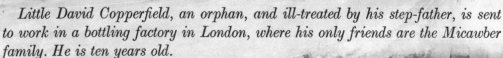

Little David Copperfield, an orphan, and ill-treated by his step-father, is sent to work in a bottling factory in London, where his only friends are the Micawber family. He is ten years old.

MR. and Mrs. Micawber and their family were going away from London, and a parting between us was near at hand. I had grown so accustomed to the Micawbers, and was so utterly friendless without them, that I felt my life was unendurable. It was in my walk home one night and the sleepless hours which followed when I lay in bed, that the thought first occurred to me to run away. To go, by some means or other, down into the country, to the only relation I had in the world, and tell my story to my aunt, Miss Betsey Trotwood.

As I did not even know where Miss Betsey lived, I wrote a letter to my old nurse, Peggotty, asking her if she remembered, and saying I had a particular occasion for half-a-guinea; and that if she could lend me that sum until I could repay it, I should be very much obliged to her, and would tell her afterwards what I had wanted it for.

Peggotty's answer soon arrived, and was, as usual, full of affection. She enclosed the half-guinea and told me that Miss Betsey lived near Dover.

I resolved to set out at the end of that week.

My box was still at my old lodging and I looked about me for some one who would help me to carry it to the booking-office. There was a long-legged young man with a very little empty donkey-cart, standing in the Blackfriars Road, whose eye I caught as I was going by. I asked whether he might or might not like a job.

"Wot job?" said the long-legged young man.

"To move a box," I answered.

"Wot box?" said the long-legged young man.

I told him mine, which was down that street there, and which I wanted him to take to the Dover coach-office for sixpence.

"Done with you for a tanner!" said the long-legged young man, and directly got upon his cart and rattled away at such a rate, that it was as much as I could do to keep pace with the donkey.

There was a defiant manner about this young man that I did not much like; as the bargain was made, however, I took him upstairs to the room I was leaving, and we brought the box down and put it on his cart; and he rattled away as if he, my box, the cart, and the donkey, were all equally mad; and I was quite out of breath with calling and running after him, when I caught him at the coach-office.

Being much flushed and excited, I tumbled my half-guinea out of my pocket; so I put it in my mouth for safety, and had just tied the direction-card on my box when I felt myself violently chucked under the chin by the long-legged young man, and saw my half-guinea fly out of my mouth into his hand.

"You give me my money back, if you please," said I, very much frightened; but he jumped into the cart, sat upon my box, and rattled away harder than ever.

I ran after him as fast as I could. "Give me my box and money, will you?" I cried, bursting into tears.

I narrowly escaped being run over, twenty times at least, in half a mile. At length, confused by fright and heat, I left the young man to go where he would with my box and money; and, panting and crying, but never stopping, faced about for Greenwich, which I had understood was on the Dover road.

For anything I know, I may have had some wild idea of running all the way to Dover, but I came to a stop in the Kent Road where I sat down on a door-step. It was by this time dark; I heard the clocks strike ten. But it was a summer night and fine weather. When I had recovered my breath I trudged on miserably until I happened to pass a little shop, where it was written up that ladies' and gentlemen's wardrobes were bought. The master of this shop was sitting at the door in his shirt-sleeves, smoking. I went up the next by-street, took off my waist-coat, rolled it neatly under my arm, and came back to the shop-door. "If you please, sir," I said, "I am to sell this for a fair price."

He took the waist-coat, stood his pipe upon its head against the door-post, went into the shop, followed by me, spread the waist-coat on the counter, and looked at it there, held it up against the light and looked at it there.

"What do you call a price, now, for this here little weskit?" he said.

"Would eighteenpence be—?" I hinted.

"I should rob my family if I was to offer ninepence for it," he said and gave it me back.

I said I would take ninepence for it, if he pleased. Not without some grumbling, he gave ninepence. I buttoned my jacket and set off once again, with my ninepence in my pocket.

Never shall I forget the lonely sensation of first lying down without a roof above my head! I found a haystack and lay down by it and slept until the warm beams of the sun woke me. Then I crept away and struck into the long dusty track which I knew to be the Dover road. I heard the church-bells ringing, as I plodded on; and I passed a church or two where the congregation were inside, and the sound of singing came out into the sunshine. I felt quite wicked in my dirt and dust, and with my tangled hair.

I got, that Sunday, through three-and-twenty miles, and toiling into Chatham, crept, at last, upon a sort of grass-grown battery overhanging a lane. Here I lay down and slept soundly until morning.

Very stiff and sore of foot I was in the morning, and feeling that I could go but a very little way that day, I resolved to make the sale of my jacket its principal business. It was a likely place to sell a jacket in; for the dealers in second-hand clothes were numerous. At last I found one that I thought looked promising, at the corner of a dirty lane. Into this shop I went with a palpitating heart; which was not relieved when an ugly old man, with the lower part of his face all covered with a stubbly grey beard, rushed out of a dirty den behind it, and seized me by the hair of my head. He was a dreadful old man to look at, in a filthy flannel waistcoat, and smelling terribly of rum.

"Oh, what do you want?" he said. "Oh, my eyes and limbs, what do you want? Oh, my lungs and liver, what do you want? Oh, goroo, goroo!"

"I wanted to know," I said, trembling, "if you would buy a jacket."

"Oh, let's see the jacket!" cried the old man. "Oh, my heart on fire, show the jacket to us!"

With that he took his trembling hands, which were like the claws of a great bird, out of my hair.

"Oh, how much for the jacket?" cried the old man, after examining it. "Oh, goroo!—how much for the jacket?"

"Half-a-crown," I answered.

"Oh, my lungs and liver," cried the old man, "no! Oh, my eyes, no! Oh, my limbs, no! Eighteenpence. Goroo!"

"Well," said I, "I'll take eighteenpence."

"Oh, my liver!" cried the old man, throwing the jacket on a shelf. "Get out of the shop! Oh, my lungs, get out of the shop! Oh, my eyes and limbs—goroo!"

I never was so frightened in my life, before or since. So I went outside and sat down in the shade in a corner. And I sat there so many hours that the shade became sunlight, and the sunlight became shade again, and still I sat there waiting for the money. He made many attempts to induce me to consent to an exchange; at one time coming out with a fishing-rod, at another with a fiddle, at another with a cocked hat, at another with a flute. But I sat there in desperation; each time asking him, with tears in my eyes, for my money or my jacket. At last he began to pay me in halfpence at a time; and was full two hours getting by easy stages to a shilling.

"Oh, my eyes and limbs!" he then cried, "will you go for twopence more?"

"I can't," I said; "I shall be starved."

"Oh, my lungs and liver, will you go for threepence?"

"I would go for nothing, if I could," I said, "but I want the money badly."

"Oh, go—roo! Will you go for fourpence?"

I was so faint and weary that I closed with this offer; and taking the money out of his claw, went away more hungry and thirsty than I had ever been, a little before sunset. But at an expense of threepence I soon refreshed myself completely; and being in better spirits then, limped seven miles upon my road.

My bed at night was under another haystack, where I rested comfortably, after having washed my blistered feet in a stream. When I took the road again next morning, I found that it lay through hop-grounds and orchards. The orchards were ruddy with ripe apples, and in a few places the hop-pickers were already at work. I thought it all extremely beautiful, and made up my mind to sleep among the hops that night.

There were many trampers on the road next day. Some of them were most ferocious-looking ruffians, who stared at me as I went by. One young fellow, a tinker, roared to me in such a tremendous voice to come back, that I halted and looked round.

"Where are you going?" said the tinker, gripping my shirt with his blackened hand.

"I am going to Dover," I said.

"Where do you come from?" asked the tinker, giving his hand another turn in my shirt, to hold me more securely.

"I come from London," I said.

He made as though to strike me, then looked at me from head to foot.

"What do you mean," said the tinker, "by wearing my brother's silk hand-kercher? Give it over here!" And he had mine off my neck in a moment.

This adventure frightened me so, that, afterwards, when I saw any of these people coming, I turned back until I could find a hiding-place, where I remained until they had gone out of sight.

I came at last upon the bare, wide downs near Dover; and on the sixth day of my flight, there I stood with my ragged shoes, and my dusty, sunburnt, half-clothed figure, in the place so long desired.

I inquired about my aunt among the boatmen first; then the fly-drivers and the shopkeepers. I was sitting on the step of an empty shop at a street-corner, near the market-place, when a fly-driver, coming by with his carriage, dropped a horse-cloth. As I handed it up, I asked him if he could tell me where Miss Trotwood lived; though I had asked the question so often, that it almost died upon my lips.

"Old lady?" said he.

"Yes," I said, "rather."

"Pretty stiff in the back?" said he.

"Yes," I said. "I should think it very likely."

"Gruffish and comes down upon you sharp?"

My heart sank within me.

"Why then, I tell you what," said he. "If you go up there," pointing with his whip towards the heights, "and keep right on till you come to some houses facing the sea, I think you'll hear of her. My opinion is, she won't stand anything, so here's a penny for you."

I accepted the gift thankfully, and bought a loaf with it. I went in the direction my friend had indicated, and at length I saw a little shop and inquired if they could tell me where Miss Trotwood lived. A young woman, who was buying some rice, turned round quickly.

"My mistress?" she said. "What do you want with her, boy?"

"I want," I replied, "to speak to her, if you please."

My aunt's maid put her rice in a little basket and walked out of the shop; telling me that I could follow her. I followed the young woman, and we soon came to a very neat little cottage.

"This is Miss Trotwood's," said the young woman. "Now you know," and left me standing at the garden-gate.

I lifted up my eyes to the window above where I saw a pleasant-looking gentleman, who shut up one eye, nodded his head at me several times, laughed,

and went away. Then there came out of the house a lady with a handkerchief tied over her cap, and a pair of gardening gloves on her hands. I knew her immediately to be Miss Betsey, for she came stalking out of the house exactly as my poor mother had so often described her.

"Go away!" said Miss Betsey, shaking her head. "Go along! No boys here!"

With my heart at my lips, I went softly in and stood beside her as she stooped to dig up some little root.

"If you please, ma'am," I began.

She started and looked up.

"If you please, aunt."

"EH?" exclaimed Miss Betsey, in a tone of amazement.

"If you please, aunt, I am your nephew."

My aunt sat flat down on the garden-path. She stared at me until I began to cry; when she got up in a great hurry, collared me, and took me into the parlour. As I was quite unable to control my sobs, she put me on the sofa, exclaiming at intervals, "Mercy on us!"

After a time she rang the bell. "Janet," said my aunt when her servant came in. "Go upstairs, give my compliments to Mr. Dick, and say I wish to speak to him." The gentleman who had squinted at me from the upper window came in laughing.

"Mr. Dick," said my aunt, "don't be a fool."

The gentleman was serious immediately.

"Mr. Dick," said my aunt, "you have heard me mention David Copperfield."

"David Copperfield?" said Mr. Dick, who did not appear to me to remember much about it. "Oh, yes, to be sure. David, certainly."

"Well," said my aunt, "this is his boy—his son, and he has done a pretty piece of business. He has run away. Now, the question I put to you is, what shall I do with him?"

"What shall you do with him?" said Mr. Dick, feebly, scratching his head. "Oh! do with him?"

"Yes," said my aunt, with a grave look, and her forefinger held up. "Come! I want some very sound advice."

"Why, if I was you," said Mr. Dick, considering, "I should—I should wash him!"

"Janet," said my aunt, "Mr. Dick sets us all right. Heat the bath!"

The bath was a great comfort. For I began to feel pains in my limbs from lying out in the fields, and was now so tired that I could hardly keep myself awake for five minutes together. When I had bathed, they dressed me in a shirt and a pair of trousers belonging to Mr. Dick, and tied me up in two or three great shawls. What sort of bundle I looked like, I don't know, but I felt a very hot one. Feeling also very faint and drowsy, I soon lay down on the sofa again and fell asleep.

We dined soon after I awoke, off a roast fowl and a pudding; I sitting at table, not unlike a trussed bird myself, and moving my arms with considerable difficulty. All this time, I was deeply anxious to know what my aunt was going to do with me; but she took her dinner in silence, except when she fixed her eyes on me sitting opposite and said, "Mercy upon us!"

Afterwards, we sat at the window until dusk, when Janet set candles on the table, and pulled down the blinds.

"Now, Mr. Dick," said my aunt, with her grave look. "I am going to ask you another question. Look at this child."

"David's son?" said Mr. Dick, with a puzzled face.

"Exactly so," returned my aunt. "What would you do with him, now?"

"Do with David's son," said Mr. Dick. "Oh! Yes. Do with—I should put him to bed."

"Janet!" cried my aunt. "Mr. Dick sets us all right. If the bed is ready, we'll take him up to it."

The room was a pleasant one, at the top of the house, overlooking the sea, on which the moon was shining brilliantly. After I had said my prayers, and the candle had burnt out, I remember how I still sat looking at the moonlight on the water, as if I could hope to read my fortune in it. I remember how I turned my eyes away, and the feeling of gratitude which the sight of the white-curtained bed and the snow-white sheets inspired. I remember how I thought of all the solitary places under the night sky where I had slept, and how I prayed that I never might be houseless any more. I remember how I seemed to float down the moonlit glory of that track upon the sea, away into the world of dreams.

FAVOURITE POEMS

Contents

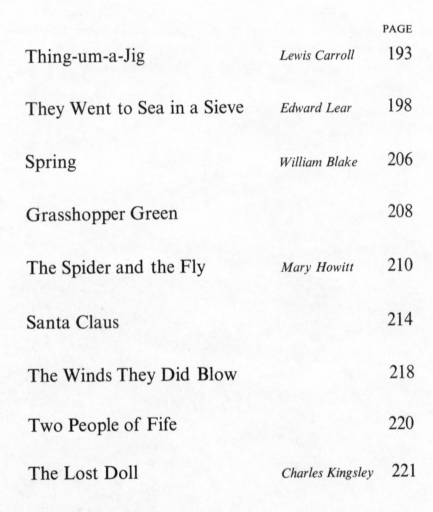

		PAGE
Thing-um-a-Jig	*Lewis Carroll*	193
They Went to Sea in a Sieve	*Edward Lear*	198
Spring	*William Blake*	206
Grasshopper Green		208
The Spider and the Fly	*Mary Howitt*	210
Santa Claus		214
The Winds They Did Blow		218
Two People of Fife		220
The Lost Doll	*Charles Kingsley*	221

These illustrated poems first appeared in
Hilda Boswell's TREASURY OF POETRY
(Two People of Fife *is taken from*
TREASURY OF CHILDREN'S STORIES)

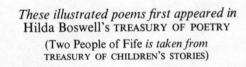

THING-UM-A-JIG

"JUST the place for a Snark!" the Bellman cried,
    As he landed his crew with care;
Supporting each man on the top of the tide
    By a finger entwined in his hair.

" Just the place for a Snark ! I have said it twice :
    That alone should encourage the crew.
Just the place for a Snark ! I have said it thrice :
    What I tell you three times is true."

The crew was complete : it included a Boots—
    A maker of Bonnets and Hoods—
A Barrister, brought to arrange their disputes—
    And a Broker to value their goods.

There was one who was famed for the number
    of things
  He forgot when he entered the ship:
His umbrella, his watch, all his jewels and rings,
  And the clothes he had bought for the trip.

He had forty-two boxes, all carefully packed,
  With his name painted clearly on each :
But, since he omitted to mention the fact,
  They were all left behind on the beach.

The loss of his clothes hardly mattered, because
   He had seven coats on when he came,
With three pair of boots—but the worst of it was,
   He had wholly forgotten his name.

He would answer to " Hi ! " or to any loud cry,
   Such as " Fry me ! " or " Fritter my wig ! "
To "What you-may-call-um! " or "What-was-his-
     name ! "
   But especially " Thing-um-a-jig ! "

While, for those who preferred a more forcible word,
  He had different names from these :
His intimate friends called him " Candle-ends,"
  And his enemies " Toasted-cheese."

" His form is ungainly—his intellect small—"
  (So the Bellman would often remark)
" But his courage is perfect ! And that, after all,
  Is the thing that one needs with a Snark."

THEY WENT TO SEA IN A SIEVE

THEY went to sea in a Sieve, they did,
  In a Sieve they went to sea ;
In spite of all their friends could say,
On a winter's morn, on a stormy day,
  In a Sieve they went to sea!
And when the Sieve turned round and round,
And everyone cried, " You'll all be drowned !"
They cried aloud, " Our Sieve ain't big,
But we don't care a button, we don't care a fig !
  In a Sieve we'll go to sea ! "
Far and few, far and few,
Are the lands where the Jumblies live ;
Their heads are green and their hands are blue,
  And they went to sea in a Sieve.

They sailed away in a Sieve, they did,
    In a Sieve they sailed so fast,
With only a beautiful pea-green veil
Tied with a riband, by way of a sail,
    To a small tobacco-pipe mast;
And everyone said who saw them go,
" Oh, won't they be soon upset, you know !
For the sky is dark, and the voyage is long,
And, happen what may, it's extremely wrong
    In a Sieve to sail so fast ! "

The water it soon came in, it did,
    The water it soon came in ;
So to keep them dry they wrapped their feet
In a pinky paper all folded neat,
    And they fastened it down with a pin.
And they passed the night in a crockery jar,
And each of them said, " How wise we are !
Though the sky be dark, and the voyage be long,
Yet we never can think we were rash or wrong
    While round in our Sieve we spin ! "

And all night long they sailed away ;
　　And when the sun went down
They whistled and warbled a moony song,
To the echoing sound of a coppery gong,
　　In the shade of the mountains brown.
" O Timballo ! How happy we are
When we live in a Sieve and a crockery jar,
And all night long in the moonlight pale
We sail away in a pea-green veil
　　In the shade of the mountains brown ! "

They sailed to the Western Sea, they did,
    To a land all covered with trees,
And they bought an Owl, and a useful Cart,
And a pound of Rice, and a Cranberry Tart,
    And a hive of Silvery Bees.
And they bought a Pig, and some green Jackdaws,
And a lovely Monkey with lollipop paws,
And forty bottles of Ring-Bo-Ree,
    And no end of Stilton Cheese.

And in twenty years they all came back,
In twenty years or more,
And everyone said, "How tall they've grown!"
For they've been to the Lakes, and the Torrible Zone,
And the hills of the Chankly Bore!"

And they drank their health, and gave them a feast
Of dumplings made of beautiful yeast;
And everyone said, " If we only live,
We, too, will go to sea in a Sieve—
    To the hills of the Chankly Bore!"

Far and few, far and few,
    Are the lands where the Jumblies live ;
Their heads are green and their hands are blue,
    And they went to sea in a Sieve.

SPRING

SOUND the flute !
　Now it's mute.
Birds delight
Day and night ;
Nightingale
In the dale,
Lark in sky,
Merrily,
Merrily, merrily to welcome in the year.

Little boy,
Full of joy ;
Little girl,
Sweet and small ;
Cock does crow,
So do you ;
Merry voice,
Infant noise,
Merrily, merrily to welcome in the year.

Little lamb,
Here I am ;
Come and lick
My white neck ;
Let me pull
Your soft wool;
Let me kiss
Your soft face :
Merrily, merrily, we welcome in the year.

GRASSHOPPER GREEN

GRASSHOPPER Green is a comical chap;
    He lives on the best of fare.
Bright little trousers, jacket and cap,
    These are his summer wear.
Out in the meadow he loves to go,
    Playing away in the sun;
It's hopperty, skipperty, high and low,
    Summer's the time for fun.

Grasshopper Green has a quaint little house ;
　　It's under the hedge so gay.
Grandmother Spider, as still as a mouse,
　　Watches him over the way.
Gladly he's calling the children, I know,
　　Out in the beautiful sun ;
It's hopperty, skipperty, high and low,
　　Summer's the time for fun.

HOPPER COT

THE SPIDER AND THE FLY

" WILL you walk into my parlour ? "
    said the Spider to the Fly ;
'Tis the prettiest little parlour that ever you did spy ;
The way into my parlour is up a winding stair,
And I have many curious things to show
    when you are there,"
" Oh, no, no," said the little Fly ;
    " to ask me is in vain ;
For who goes up your winding stair
    can ne'er come down again."

" I'm sure you must be weary, dear,
    with soaring up so high ;
Will you rest upon my little bed ? "
    said the Spider to the Fly.
" There are pretty curtains drawn around ;
    the sheets are fine and thin ;
And if you like to rest awhile,
    I'll snugly tuck you in ! "
" Oh, no, no," said the little Fly ; " for I've often
    heard it said,
They never wake again who sleep upon your bed! "

Said the cunning Spider to the Fly :
 " Dear friend, what can I do
To prove the warm affection
 I have *always* felt for you ?
I have within my pantry good store of all that's nice;
I'm sure you're very welcome—
 will you please to take a slice ? "
" Oh, no, no," said the little Fly ;
" kind sir, that cannot be ;
I've heard what's in your pantry,
 and I do not wish to see ! "

" Sweet creature ! " said the Spider,
    "you are witty and you're wise ;
How handsome are your gauzy wings,
    how brilliant are your eyes !
I have a little looking-glass
    upon my parlour shelf,
If you'll step in one moment, dear,
    you shall behold yourself."
" I thank you, gentle sir," she said,
    " for what you're pleased to say,
And bidding you good-morning now,
    I'll call another day. . . . "

SANTA CLAUS

HE comes in the night ! He comes in the night !
  He softly, silently comes ;
While the little brown heads on the pillows so white
Are dreaming of bugles and drums.
He cuts through the snow like a whip through the
  foam,
While the white flakes around whirl ;
Who tells him I know not, but he findeth the home
Of each good little boy and girl.